ALSO BY
ELISABETH RUSSELL TAYLOR

I is *Another*

Pillion Riders

Mother Country

Divide and Rule

Swann Song

TOMORROW

Elisabeth Russell Taylor

DAUNT BOOKS

First published in Great Britain in 2018 by
Daunt Books
83 Marylebone High Street
London W1U 4QW

1

A CIP catalogue record for this title is available from the British Library.

ISBN 978-1-911547-12-9

Text design and typesetting by Tetragon, London
Printed and bound by T J International Ltd, Padstow, Cornwall

www.dauntbookspublishing.co.uk

INTRODUCTION

My first experience of Elisabeth Russell Taylor's work was the short story 'Les Amants', which appears in her collection *Belated*. It is a deeply touching and resonant story, which opens with the background detail of a small community haunted by a tragic crime of which 'succeeding generations continued to bear the weight', their village becoming 'a continual reminder of the past'. The village is perched above the river Seine, the houses gouged out of the chalk cliffs. The protagonist, an inhabitant of the village since she was eighteen, is now seventy. The death of her lover has left her with no appetite for eating or socialising; she has been finding it hard to sleep. 'How to invest life with meaning when the heart had been torn from it?'

Russell Taylor's novel *Tomorrow* could be asking the same question, except that there is a far greater wound at the centre of this story. The protagonist, Elisabeth Danziger, is driven only by a determination to keep the vow she and her childhood sweetheart made before the outbreak of the Second World War: to return every August to the same place, so that in due course they would be reunited. Even though she has long since abandoned hope, 'She must not give in. If she could no longer rise to an adventurous life of the spirit, she could keep doggedly on.' This zestless persistence is reminiscent of a line halfway through the novel, in which Elisabeth Danziger recalls someone saying 'that playing patience was the nearest thing to being dead.'

Making her annual visit to the Danish island of Møn, Miss Danziger is excessively regular in her habits. She and the hotelier Fru Møller are courteous to one another; Elisabeth pretends not to notice Fru Møller's 'absurdities'. Tea is taken in the drawing room, a gong is sounded for dinner, everyone eats the same main course, coffee is taken in the study and conversation is 'orchestrated'. Lurking at the edges of this order and propriety is a churning and potentially overwhelming darkness that is all the more terrible for the contrast. This deceptively cool style brackets Elisabeth Russell Taylor with some of my favourite writers: Anita Brookner, Penelope Fitzgerald, Muriel Spark and Edith Wharton spring to mind.

In fiction, the seashore is frequently a threshold not only between land and sea but between what the land represents – order; social and personal stability – and what the sea represents – chaos; social or personal breakdown. There is a connection, too, between the sea and the past. W. H. Auden wrote of the sea as 'that state of barbaric vagueness and disorder out of which civilisation has emerged and into which, unless saved by the effort of gods and men, it is always liable to relapse.' The sea encroaches, eroding or flooding the land. In seaside narratives, there is an undermining of society and sense of self. In BBC Radio 4's *Open Book*, in a programme on the topic of 'Literary Landscape:

The Coast', Dr Alicia Rix suggested that if literature has technically 'moved on from the age of sea monsters,' these monsters have perhaps 'only been replaced with psychological demons.'

On the small island of Møn, Elisabeth Danziger is closely surrounded by sea. We feel the intense pull – the inescapable undertow – of the past. The first chapter begins in the present, in September 1960, but we soon find ourselves back in the inter-war years, in which two young Aryan German men who teach at a German university marry Jewish twins. Although living in Germany, in apartments close to the university, the couples also establish houses on Møn, which is near the German coast, and visit during the university holidays. Meanwhile, Germany's soil is 'being raked over for an unprecedented crop of anti-semitism'. Professors Jurgen Danziger and Horst Eberhardt are considered 'tainted by association through their wives': social invitations from their colleagues are scarce, and as the Second World War approaches, they find their teaching duties curtailed. The two couples begin to spend less time in their German apartments and more time on the island of Møn.

Chapter two, as if making an effort to stay in the present, begins again in the autumn of 1960, and yet already we have stepped back a little way into the past. As Elisabeth Danziger arrives at the hotel, The Tamarisks, her suitcase brushes up against the foliage at her side, 'dispersing pungent, dank summer scents that instantaneously prised open the veins of memory', and we understand that we, along with Elisabeth, like F. Scott Fitzgerald's 'boats against the current', are going to be 'borne back ceaselessly into the past'. From this recent past, Elisabeth – in an image that almost makes me feel the cold seawater filling her lungs – is 'lured . . . deeper and deeper back, down, into the past'.

Elisabeth is in the yellow room, where her suitcase slumps 'thin and old', so that the yellow seems sickly. It is difficult to take in this detail without Charlotte Perkins Gilman's yellow wallpaper coming to mind, the 'things in that paper that nobody knows but me, or ever will'; the woman or many women creeping about behind the pattern, trapped within it; the sense of suppressed yet overwhelming mental anguish. This association reminds me of a sequence in Janet Frame's autobiography, in which the hated Miss Low and her 'castor oil from the hated slim, blue glass bottle' are echoed in 'Miss Botting, a woman in a blue costume the same colour as the castor-oil bottle'. What might otherwise be an innocent blue now connotes what is hated; Charlotte Perkins Gilman's yellow evokes not beautiful yellow things 'like buttercups, but old foul, bad yellow things.' Elisabeth Danziger's troublingly yellow room faces the 'grumous' sea; the seaweed-scented air gets into her lungs and caught in the curtains; salt clings insistently to her face. We have, in this layering of imagery, a keen sense of a traumatic and tenacious past.

We are acutely aware of the sea throughout this novel. In the opening sentence, the sea is being watched. It is a 'menacing sea: potentially dangerous, urged on by the tide, looking for a killing.' It 'has encroached all round the coast' of the flat island. A long-awaited letter has an envelope 'the colour of today's sea', as if this 'dark and leaden' sea could soak into anything and everything. The narrative itself is bracketed by the sea, enclosed by 'the bice waters of the Baltic' and the sweeping waves. It is on this island that seems so vulnerable to the rapacious sea that the Danziger and Eberhardt children, cousins and lovers Elisabeth and Daniel, hear that the war is coming, that it is imminent. Decades later, Elisabeth observes that Møn has been violated by the sea: 'The land had been raped years past by the sea. All that remained on the barren expanse was a deafening silence.' In this description, we also recognise Elisabeth herself, who 'never spoke about her feelings'.

There is, then, a suggestion of psychological disturbance, which becomes manifest on the occasions when Elisabeth is overwhelmed by 'an intolerable weight of memory; not that of individual occasions but of the entire past'. Visiting the island's museum, she suffers an auditory hallucination: 'This dreadful invasion was one with which she was familiar: something between a hum and a buzz, and terrifying for being unresponsive to any attempt to silence it. She must wait. She must wait – as she had to when pursued by the sound at night – for it to pass.' She hears her own voice cry out, 'A mine!' In the church, when an ancient Hebrew word meaning 'it would have been enough!' rises from her, she is at first unaware that the word emanated from herself. In the garden at The Tamarisks, when a wail of 'Mutti!' begins to rise to the surface, she stuffs a handkerchief into her mouth to suppress it. On her trip to look at frescos that interpret the story of the Massacre of the Innocents, the slaughter of children, she closes her eyes, as in the museum, 'and, as she did so, valves that normally regulated memory burst open. It was terrible: pure pain.'

Like Elisabeth, the reader must then witness at close quarters the most terrible act, the unbearable trauma at the heart of *Tomorrow*. In that moment, 'Life in progress has ceased. Time has stopped.' The difficulty of continuing in the present is echoed in Elisabeth's difficulty in swallowing her food; more than once she almost chokes on her meals. 'My body gets itself into a state of refusal,' she explains. 'Life "sticks in my throat", I suppose.'

It is pertinent that The Tamarisks was Elisabeth Danziger's childhood home before the war, and remains unchanged. 'It was a relief to know that the house had not been depleted and that it remained uncontaminated. Elisabeth never craved to remove items; to take anything away from The Tamarisks would be, she felt, to disfigure a perfectly beautiful body.' At this point in the narrative, the significance of the metaphor is painfully apparent.

The past inhabits nooks and crannies. At The Tamarisks, in a small dusty box in 'the subterranean depths' beneath the bath, Elisabeth has kept a fossil, one of a dozen items secreted in adult-proof places by the cousins in childhood, before the war: 'It'll be wonderful to have a treasure-hunt when we eventually return!' The past possesses people; they get stuck. At the hotel, a female guest nearing seventy behaves like a little girl, having 'resolutely refused to emerge' from childhood; playing with dolls, Bo-Bo is 'drawn back in the slip-stream of time to her ecstatic infancy'. Meanwhile Bo-Bo's husband comes annually to Møn for the moths and fossils. The past is where life really dwells; 'what was alive of Daniel was their past together and her memories of it'.

There is a poignant anecdote about a blind woman who had, on the wall of her cottage, a seascape painted by her father, 'a thick impasto of raging waves'. After taking down the painting and donating it to the museum, the artist hung a papier mâché tray in its place, so that his daughter would 'not feel the absence of the picture.' Where once the sea raged, the papier mâché tray hangs blankly, infused with no meaning other than to be where *something* is expected to be, filling the space.

The idea of 'tomorrow' is significant of course, and punctuates the narrative. 'Tomorrow,' Fru Møller says to Elisabeth, 'we're promised fine weather'; 'Tomorrow . . . ' say the guests, anticipating a fishing expedition. But in the morning, it is raining heavily; there is thunder and lightning: 'What they had wanted was to have gone on a fishing expedition. Such a delightful prospect! And now this had happened! It might blight the whole of their stay . . . ' Back in 1939, Elisabeth and Daniel plan a recital that is to 'both begin and close with Strauss's *Morgen*.' Lines from Mackay's poem – *Und morgen wird die Sonne wieder scheinen: And tomorrow the sun will shine again* – repeat through the novel like the voice that keeps trying to rise in Elisabeth, like something briefly seen through cracks and gaps in the present-day narrative, like the 'grey shroud of sky . . . torn in places to reveal streaks of blood red and aquamarine blue.' We find the poem in full at the beginning and at the end of the novel, and lines from it at the beginning and at the end of Elisabeth's stay. In this beautifully structured novel, lives go unlived, rendezvous are missed, messages are delayed or undelivered. 'You see,' Elisabeth says to Daniel, as they plan the recital and the performance of the Strauss piece, 'by *starting* with it you emphasise the wholly hopeful, optimistic expectations the words imply and then, by *ending* with it, you can stress the double-edged sword quality: the irony. It's hopeless trying to plan for tomorrow'.

Year after year, Elisabeth makes this journey to the island, stays at the same hotel, in her usual room, and keeps so strictly to the same itinerary that it would be possible 'to forecast precisely where she will be on the island at any moment of her stay'. The repetition is reminiscent of a ghost story in which a spirit makes some journey or performs some action over and over again. Elisabeth is compelled to do this even though it causes her mind to 'swell with memories' so that she 'feared the bounds of her mind would burst and she would be swamped, her sanity irretrievable in the flood damage.' Like the sea that surrounds her, the past is vast and ever-present. It is in a room that appears 'oceanic' that the heart-wrenching ending takes place.

There are brutal and vivid images in the novel that remain with me. When revisited and reconsidered, the description of 'a stone the dimensions of a child's bicycle wheel, in which a huge ammonite was embedded' brought tears to my eyes. In a novel so concerned with the way in which the past hangs around to haunt us, it is fitting that *Tomorrow* itself should linger so disquietingly in the reader's mind.

ALISON MOORE, 2018

TOMORROW

TOMORROW

MORGEN

Und morgen wird die Sonne wieder scheinen
Und auf dem Wege, den ich gehen werde,
Wird uns, die Glücklichen, sie wieder einen
Inmitten dieser sonnenatmenden Erde ...

Und zu dem Strand, dem weiten, wogenblauen,
Werden wir still und langsam niedersteigen,
Stumm werden wir uns in die Augen schauen,
Und auf uns sinkt des Glückes stummes Schweigen ...

And tomorrow the sun will shine again
and on the path we walk in our happiness
it will again unite us
in the midst of this sun-breathing earth ...

And to the wide shore with its blue waves
we shall again descend, slow and still,
mutely we shall look into each other's eyes
and the silence of happiness will again sink upon us ...

JOHN HENRY MACKAY
English translation by S.S. Prawer
Music by Richard Strauss

PREFACE

Denmark was occupied by the German army on 9 April 1940. The steadfast behaviour of the Danish authorities and the unanimous opinion of the Danish people persuaded the Germans not to molest the Jews. However, in September 1943 the mounting efforts of the Danish Resistance movement led to martial law being declared. With it the position of the Jews became dangerous.

A popular movement for the rescue of the whole Jewish population was launched. Within three weeks 7,200 Jews were smuggled to safety in neutral Sweden. Five hundred Jews, ignorant of the plan for their rescue, were seized by the Nazis and sent to Theresienstadt where they remained until the spring of 1945. The intervention of the Swedish Red Cross resulted in their being removed to Sweden.

At the end of the war the Jews returned to Denmark. They found their businesses and their houses intact. The stewardship of ordinary Danish people had been exemplary.

Less than two per cent of Danish Jews perished.

SEPTEMBER 1960

Fru Møller was unusually aware as she gazed out over the bice waters of the Baltic not only of their tone but of their texture. Like them she was feeling dark and leaden. She had been waiting for a letter from London for three weeks, in reply to one from her requiring an immediate answer. Her frustration was mounting. But she had no alternative but to wait; if she wrote again, asking the unknown woman for a response by return of post, she might positively encourage further delay.

The familiar sight of the sea did nothing to console her. Its familiarity reinforced in her a sense of boundless monotony. She watched the waters gently move in a single mind, their purpose to consume and conceal.

It was several seconds before the sound of turning wheels on the gravel impressed itself upon Fru Møller's consciousness and lent her the energy to turn her back on the ocean. Facing inland she managed: 'Good-day, Mr Olson. I think we're due for rain.'

'Well, your season's over now, I imagine!'

Indeed. And perhaps for all time. Fru Møller sighed inwardly as she walked slowly across the terrace, into the house, shuffling through the letters the postman had handed her. There was, at last, a letter with an English stamp, franked London SW7. The envelope was the colour of today's sea. The handwriting as foreboding.

The tone and contents of Lady Davis's letter added their weight to Fru Møller's depression. No other letter she had ever read had painted so unintentionally – and unflatteringly – vivid a portrait of its author.

Dear Mrs Møller,

I was quite shocked by the contents of your letter. It has taken me all these many days to recover sufficiently from your notification to collect my shattered nerves and write to you.

Miss Danziger has been in my service for fifteen years. My husband, the late Sir Albert Davis, insisted in 1945 that we offer refuge to one of the unfortunate survivors of the concentration camps. My husband was, at the time, wholly occupied with the resettlement of these people and saw the necessity of setting an example. I was adamant: I would not take in a child. I knew I could not love another's as my own, you understand. But I agreed to take in Miss Danziger because servants were all but impossible to obtain and she was of a suitable age to perform the duties of housemaid: 'An orphan who works is not lost', as we say. When, in 1956, my dear husband passed away, I moved out of Belgrave Square, where we had been camping rather uncomfortably on just two of the six floors of the house, and brought Miss Danziger here. I promoted her to housekeeper.

Despite living under the same roof as Miss Danziger for fifteen years, I can tell you little about her. You must have noticed for yourself: she was hardly prepossessing. As for her character, I would describe it as secretive, verging on the smug. I do not know anything about her background, she never mentioned it, but I did observe she spent her afternoons off differently from my English servants. She was a great *aficionado* of the museums and once a month, I believe, she attended a theatre. She had no male visitors. I would not have permitted that. She had one or two women associates – refugees like herself, I imagine. She had no family.

Miss Danziger's death comes as a surprise to me: she never had a day's ill health while in my employ. She once complained, many years ago, that she slept badly and my own doctor was kind enough to prescribe her sleeping tablets.

I have often wondered, when Miss Danziger set off for the Baltic and her annual holiday at your establishment, what particular attraction your house and your part of the world had for her. She was a woman of habit, utterly predictable – you could set your clock by her – and I assumed she liked the routine of returning to a place with which she was familiar, where she could speak German. I never permitted her to speak German with me.

I trust this information will suffice and that the Danish police will have no need to contact me. I would find any official investigations most unpleasant and

I have nothing to add to what I have stated in this letter.

Yours sincerely,

Dora Davis

And, as she came to the end of her letter, Lady Davis threw her signature across the page with a confident flourish.

'Mrs Rudge! Mrs Rudge! I would be obliged if you would drop this letter in the box at the corner of Prince Consort Road on your way home.' Lady Davis preferred her letters franked SW7 – not SW4, Mrs Rudge's postal address.

❖

It was not that she had liked Elisabeth Danziger, but theirs had been a relationship of mutual respect; their behaviour to one another had been courteous. Not once had Miss Danziger made Fru Møller feel herself an interloper at The Tamarisks. Not once had her special relationship with the house led her to make any privileged demand. It could not be said that she had contributed very positively to the social life at the small hotel; on the other hand she could not have been accused of detracting from it. Fru Møller's sentiments were being marshalled within her, armed to defend Miss Danziger who, it was common knowledge, had had a tragic life. And even if that had not been the case her obvious affection for Møn, and her gratitude to the Danish people as a whole, would have been sufficient to arouse in Fru Møller a sense of willing obligation towards her guest. So! She too had been a servant in a household that did not understand and respect the responsibilities attached to the relationship between master and servant. Before Fru Møller (widowed six months after an unconsummated marriage) had found her present job, she had suffered something of the sort herself. What a pity Miss Danziger had never confided in her! After all, they were both women, both single women . . .

Fru Møller climbed the stairs wearily. Bertha had stripped the bedrooms of their curtains and covers. Two rooms would require redecoration; she did not like the turquoise and hyacinth blues that a regular guest with a passion for Monet had persuaded her to apply. In Miss Danziger's yellow room the dead woman's suitcase slumped reproachfully, thin and old, as if anticipating further replenishment before making its final journey. As carefully as Bertha had packed its few contents Fru Møller unpacked them. She laid out each article on the bed. Lady Davis clearly wanted no truck with Miss Danziger's possessions; she had not bothered to refer to them, to answer Fru Møller's enquiry as to what should be done with them. Fru Møller examined closely the two sleeveless cotton blouses, the faded dirndl skirt, the peach rayon petticoat, the Westminster Public Library copy of *Mansfield Park*, the Ponds cold cream, the sponge bag, the packet of sanitary towels. The exposure of Miss Danziger's meagre possessions revealed nothing more of herself or her life than had been obvious. And nothing of her death.

Fru Møller heard Bertha on the landing: 'Bertha! Pack these things up for me again, my dear . . . And put the case in the cupboard for the time being.' As the girl entered the room Fru Møller left it, calling back, 'I've heard from

London. The woman with whom poor Miss Danziger lived was her *employer* . . . ' And while she counted the freshly washed and ironed linen and stacked it neatly in the linen cupboard on the landing, she continued, 'She throws no light on Miss Danziger, only on herself; she sounds perfectly frightful.' There was a pause; Fru Møller counted sheets on the top shelf: ' . . . thirty-three, thirty-four. I'll let the commissioner have the letter and when he gives us the go-ahead to dispose of these things, you may like to take them down to the seamen's mission.'

❖

It was in 1927 that the Danziger and Eberhardt families formalised their interdependence with the purchase of two houses on a small island at the extreme south-east corner of Denmark's five hundred island possessions. They had no particular reason for choosing Møn except that it was near the German coast and hence more accessible to them. The island was singularly without pretension; just a modest chrysalis-shaped piece of undulating pasture, arable and marshland – a place ignored by those who required drama of an obvious kind. The whole island had the charm of a personal garden; nowhere was the hand – delicate and caring – of man absent. Even the remote corners and places left wild seemed to have been included in a plan to preserve something wild: they had not been ignored.

The stated purpose of the Danzigers and the Eberhardts was to provide for themselves a quiet environment away from the university in which to pursue their interests: a place where the twin sisters – the wives of the two men – would be content, and their children free, occupied and together. The underlying purpose – barely perceived and never avowedly expressed – was more far-reaching; both families sensed that if they were to survive the increasing political chaos that had resulted from the Treaty of Versailles, if their relationship was to flourish and find regeneration in their children, they might need at some future date to transplant themselves from the infected soil of Germany and put down roots in the more wholesome Danish pasture.

They did not set out with preconceptions, but finding two magnificent houses – one in the English and the other in the Italian mode – and being in the fortunate position of having abundant funds, they made their purchases quickly and joyously.

The Tamarisks was poised on a promontory with views over the Baltic on three sides. It had been designed for an Englishman at the turn of the century by the architect Edwin Lutyens, in his predominantly Elizabethan style. It consisted of an H-shaped block with a huge central Hall with double height space and a small minstrels' gallery just large enough to accommodate a string quartet. In place of Elizabethan long galleries, more modest corridors – off which bedrooms and bathrooms were located – overlooked the Hall through magnificently carved balustrades. A concealed staircase led down from the bedroom floor to the kitchens and up to the servants' quarters. A flamboyant staircase with banisters carved to complement the features on the balustrades led out of the Hall to the first floor.

Lutyens had supervised every detail of the design of the house. The weathered brick he had insisted upon had had to be collected from houses fallen into ruin all over Denmark; the mellow tones were required by him not only for the exterior, so that the house would blend perfectly into the colours of its setting, but also for the interior – for the Hall, study, library and dining-room, where the walls were to be left unfinished and only the ceilings plastered and painted white or embellished with strap-work. For those public rooms he designed imposing fireplaces six and eight feet wide, and individual fire-guards and fire irons. Each of the doors of the public rooms was hewn from Latvian oak and finished with iron door furniture that echoed the designs chosen for the fire-irons. The architect might well have wished, had he been able, to paint the pictures and embroider the wall hangings he sketched in on his plans. Failing this, however, he contented himself by suggesting appropriate works of art; his advice was taken and when the house changed hands many of the pictures and tapestries were left in situ. The estate agents advertised The Tamarisks as 'An Englishman's Castle'. None but a pedant would have argued with the description.

Outside, in the areas enclosed by the H-shaped plan, Lutyens designed gravelled terraces as formal gardens in which he placed stone benches for tables and seats, and urns. With the exceptions of a yellow climbing rose with shining evergreen leaves called 'Mermaid' – chosen as much for its name as its exquisite blooms – on the north face of the house, and a fragrant wisteria that snaked across the south face, all shrubs and flowers were rooted in the urns.

Beyond the north terrace lay a walled garden in which fruit, vegetables and flowers were grown for the table; and there was a pleasure garden and two tennis courts. It was bordering the path that led from the sea-facing terrace, through the dunes to the beach, that the eponymous tamarisks were planted, trees resistant to the open situation and poor sandy soil. The name The Tamarisks was not, Lutyens felt, appropriate for his creation but his client's preference prevailed and, after his untimely death and the purchase of the house by Professor Danziger and his wife, the house and its name had become indivisible on Møn.

The nearby Tuscan Villa bought by Professor Eberhardt and his wife was just that: a faded raspberry stucco building with colonnades and a tower. It had been built in the eighteenth century for an Italian merchant who, *persona non grata* in his native Sienna, sold a cargo of silks at an exorbitant profit in Scandinavia and, by making lavish gifts to absentee landlords, managed to secure himself land on Møn, where he planned to pass the final quarter of his life in tranquillity. In the event, he made himself so popular through his generosity, he became the focus of attention – but that is another story. The position occupied by the Villa was somewhat inaccessible and the Villa itself too large for any islander to run; it stood toppling into ruin for over one hundred years and when Professor Eberhardt and his wife bought it restoration meant rebuilding.

Professors Danziger and Eberhardt held chairs in English and Italian respectively, in the ancient northern German university that was the focus of the city where they had attended high school. Both men were Aryans – blond,

15

blue-eyed peasants from the Hunsrück. They had been bred to tend cattle and raise crops but from the time they had learnt to read – rather late by the standards of the city, at the age of eleven – the boys discovered more joy between the pages of books than in the fields and byres. Their private and solitary recreation first raised suspicion and then scorn in their parents and contemporaries. Reading was a difficult occupation to pursue in the Hunsrück; there were no libraries within travelling distance and no money with which to buy books. Their passion would have spent itself unfulfilled had not a master at the village school, weary of an unending succession of crass pupils, found himself enlivened by the discovery of two literate boys in his midst. He made them his protégés and supplied them with a steady stream of Walser and Kleist and Goethe, and translations of novels from the English, French and Italian. And so it was that Jurgen Danziger and Horst Eberhardt, encouraged by him, pursued their prey. It was a dangerous pursuit. The villagers regarded the boys as traitors for not farming; they might just as well have declared themselves atheists or internationalists.

Because they were made to feel aliens in their own village the boys strove to flee it. Their reading had all the effects with which reading is credited: it stimulated their curiosity, enlarged their horizons, engendered in them a literacy with which to express thoughts and feelings that they would otherwise not have known they possessed. Effectively, it took them on to a high school in a university city hundreds of miles to the north-west – a step that would prove crucial in their lives.

The boys were poor, and had had no idea of the hardships they would have to face in their quest for knowledge. They were dependent upon scholarships for their fees and obliged to accept hand-outs from the church to feed themselves. They found this degrading and by taking on menial jobs managed only to supplement these monies – not to replace them. By the time they had their first degrees they were unrivalled in their ability to live on bread, milk and roots. It was precisely this frugality, however, that attracted the sisters who were to become their wives.

The Gertler sisters, Charlotte and Anna, were the twin daughters of a wealthy Jewish industrialist. Their town house was in Baden-Baden. In addition to the house, which stood in its own park and had its own stabling, their father had a vast apartment in his office block in Frankfurt where he entertained and accommodated visiting clients, but which the family used when they attended the opera and theatre in that town. And they had a country estate, a modest *schloss*, in Bavaria. When the time came for the girls to choose a university they opted for one as far away from Baden-Baden, Frankfurt and Bavaria as they could find – but only because they felt themselves far too dependent upon their parents and their parents' wealth. They were going to the university to develop their independence as much as anything else.

Mr Gertler accompanied his wife when she set off on a reconnaissance of the university city where their daughters would be studying. Mrs Gertler had first to establish that suitable accommodation was available for her daughters and then negotiate terms. 'Suitable' was a portmanteau word in the Gertler family, thoroughly understood by all its members but which would have conveyed only a fraction of its meaning to anyone outside the family. Fortunately, suitable accommodation did not imply a mirror image of the luxury of the Gertler set-up in Baden-Baden, Frankfurt or Bavaria; it meant safe, solid comfort in the home of professional people. Mr Gertler, having been obliged to leave school at twelve and make a fortune by the age of twenty-two, in order to support a tribe of avaricious relations, had a rosy, unrealistic confidence in the suitability of lawyers, doctors and university professors; it was with such families that his daughters should lodge. Having made money easily he had no respect for others who did likewise. In a world of idiots, he never tired of saying, making money is as simple as falling pregnant. Mr Gertler had never passed an examination, never known the exquisite pleasure of being deferred to, and it was those qualifications for which he had respect.

Anna and Charlotte took greater pleasure in the company of their parents than in that of others for, if untutored, the Gertlers were unashamedly epicurean. The sisters adored their parents, whose unstinting love had provided them with absolute security and engendered in them an unerring ability to distinguish twenty-two carat sentiments from pinchbeck ones. They carried this discernment into all corners of their experience; they had no difficulty discriminating between good writing and indifferent, or between a real sense of form and colour and a contrived display. And they favoured music which did not insist upon and exaggerate the feelings it conveyed.

The Gertlers' houses were lavishly accoutred and staffed. They had been furnished by antique dealers and designed by interior decorators because, as Mr Gertler was the first to admit, neither he nor his wife could tell baroque from Biedermeier. Mr Gertler accepted that if he was to continue to make money in machine tools he was going to have to continue entertaining men impressed by the evidence of wealth. But since he was a Jew and his clients found that fact rather less to their taste, Mr Gertler – a pragmatist – was not going to be caught out on two counts: modesty and monotheism. He was not bothered by anti-semitism; 'That's their problem,' he would say, adding, 'and I don't intend it to become mine!'

Anna and Charlotte understood their parents' reasons for display, but because it was not necessary to them, they would not indulge it themselves. However, by the time that they were old enough for university their tastes were developed. The pictures they liked to look at, the clothes they chose to wear, the furniture they liked around them, and the food demanded by their palates had been informed and gratified by wealth. Horst and Jurgen, on their first invitation to the 'suitable' accommodation Mr and Mrs Gertler had leased for their daughters, were stunned by the *luxe et volupté* they encountered.

It appeared to acquaintances that it was the attraction of opposites that led to the marriages of Anna and Jurgen and Charlotte and Horst. Close friends knew otherwise. They recognised the young people as soul mates for whom life was not divided into compartments – work and leisure, pain and pleasure – but was experienced as a totality, a thread along whose length the whole of European culture, the benefits of love and friendship, the mystery of family life and childbirth were strung, indivisible from each other. Each was voracious for knowledge and experience, committed to human relationships, to the pursuit of truth and justice, and the establishment of equality. To some outside their circle it appeared charmed, and the four seemed too good to be true. Students less academically accomplished, less physically attractive, pondered what ichor it could be that flowed through their veins and lent them their smiling seriousness. Among those in Horst's and Jurgen's year were some who imagined that the lure of money must have determined their fellow students' choice. But even as the accusation formed itself, the charge appeared empty and the students had to admit that it was their own mediocrity that provoked their envy.

The Gertlers took Jurgen and Horst to their hearts. It never entered their minds that any man would court and marry either of their daughters for a reason other than love and admiration for such delightful, beautiful and intelligent young women. Nor could they understand why Horst's and Jurgen's families declined to attend the civil marriage ceremony the four shared, and the reception that followed. Mr and Mrs Gertler were so genuinely unimpressed by riches that they could not imagine that their own wealth might be overwhelming and intimidating to others. Seeing that neither Horst nor Jurgen appeared upset by the refusal of their families to attend the celebration, Mr and Mrs Gertler accepted their explanation that it was impossible for those who worked the land to leave it for twelve hours, let alone the forty-eight which would be required to travel to and from Bavaria.

Anna and Jurgen honeymooned in England; Charlotte and Horst in Italy. On their return to Germany six weeks later the couples settled into the apartments that the Gertlers had leased and had furnished for them, near the university, in the medieval centre of the city.

Horst and Jurgen had completed their postgraduate work and had been appointed to teach. Anna and Charlotte had first degrees and had opted to pursue their interests independently of the university, so as to have time to run their homes and prepare for motherhood. The closeness the twins had always felt deepened, and the two men, whose lives had been harnessed in tandem since they entered school, grew equally close. The couples discovered that they preferred the company of each other to the more communal activities associated with the university, and for a while they failed to perceive that invitations from their colleagues were few and far between. Thinking back to the Hunsrück the men remembered the extent to which their families were indivisible from their land. But they ignored the fact that German soil was being raked over for an unprecedented crop of anti-semitism; that less accomplished academics than they, jealous of their intellectual prowess and material privilege, revelled in the growing certainty that, tainted by association through their wives, the two would someday be checked.

Anna and Charlotte had been used to a background of anti-semitism and, like their parents, treated it as the problem of its perpetrators – that is until they gave birth to their children, Elisabeth and Daniel. Then a shadow fell across their well-being; they became uncharacteristically anxious. This showed itself in an over-protectiveness of their offspring. However, if at an unconscious level the sisters felt their Jewishness was going to be the most decisive determining factor in their futures and the futures of their children, such feelings were offset by the blindness assimilation brought with it. Thus they were inhibited from taking the appropriate steps to safeguard themselves.

Until 1935 the families had restricted their visits to Møn to the university vacations. After 1935 their visits became more frequent – and lengthened in time. The professors had been warned by the chancellor of the university that it might be prudent to seek work elsewhere. The chancellor was not himself a member of the National Socialists (nor were their views his); however, he was not predisposed to make a martyr of himself. After 1937, whilst he authorised the payment of the professors' salaries, he forbade them to lecture or teach on his premises.

The families continued to move between their apartments in the city, where Daniel and Elisabeth were at school, and their houses on Møn. They travelled in Italy and England but not, as might reasonably have been surmised, to seek possible employment outside Germany, or to forge relationships in more liberal countries, or even to leave valuables outside Germany, but in pursuit of works of art. They had determined that the Tuscan Villa should be truly Tuscan in every detail, and that The Tamarisks should reflect every aspect of Elizabethan taste. They were amassing pictures, furniture, manuscripts and other lesser decorative objects. The threat of chaos appeared positively to stimulate their appetite for possessions. When their parents' travels of acquisition coincided with Elisabeth's and Daniel's school holidays the two young people chose to stay on Møn rather than accompany them. Not only was the island their idyll but the freedom they experienced there was more peculiarly intoxicating as it became increasingly threatened.

In 1939 Elisabeth and Daniel were eighteen; they had been somewhat protected in school by their fathers' Aryan names and their own identification with German culture. But the connective tissue between their understanding of the political situation and the way in which it would inevitably affect them was a far more sensitive conductor than that of their parents. Yet, in their determination not to question their parents' behaviour, not to undermine Anna's and Charlotte's conviction that they would somehow be 'all right', because Horst and Jurgen would take care of everything and make it so, they too found themselves paralysed in the face of the urgent need to take action.

They discussed; they argued. Who in his right mind would want to live in America? As children they might get a visa for England but Britain was not accepting any more adults and they would not leave without their parents. There was no point in going to France or, for that matter, staying on Møn; Germany had borders with both countries and the Germans had it in mind to conquer the world. Best to stay put, where they knew they could hide, in the Hunsrück or the *schloss*. For years the Gertlers had been laying in stores at the *schloss* – and they had bought gold . . . Among old man Gertler's favourite axioms was 'every man has his price'. Above all, they would all stay together.

SUNDAY

'You'll be wanting The Tamarisks?'

'That's right! Thank you!'

The driver and the passengers on the small, local bus observed the rules: no talking while the vehicle was in motion. But while passengers alighted at the stop before Miss Danziger's, the driver had taken the opportunity to make it known to the foreign tourist that he recognised and remembered her. He drew the bus to a halt where the road joined a bush-canopied path, and it was down this path that Elisabeth Danziger walked, her suitcase brushing the foliage on her right side, dispersing pungent, dank summer scents that instantaneously prised open the veins of memory.

The terrace was deserted. Small iron tables and chairs had been vacated very recently, it appeared, for the chairs were set haphazardly and did not seem to belong to any particular table. Miss Danziger, exhausted, rested her case. The façade of The Tamarisks was wholly concealed under a haze of pale blue tresses quivering with the activity of bees. A soft lapping sound rose from the direction of the sea.

Und auf dem Wege . . .

'Miss Danziger! Miss Danziger!' a woman's voice called from the open front door. 'How nice to see you again!' Fru Møller strode across the terrace, her hand extended. 'Did you have a pleasant journey?' And without waiting for a reply she turned and called into the house, 'Bertha! Miss Danziger's arrived!'

Fru Møller's welcome and Bertha's determination to take care of her suitcase relieved Miss Danziger of the need to speak or act; it was enough simply to nod and smile.

'I noticed the bus was a little late this afternoon,' Fru Møller said, in an effort to explain why tea was no longer being served on the terrace. 'Never mind! Bertha will bring you up something on a tray. You must be very hungry.' As the three women turned into the house Elisabeth Danziger was peculiarly aware of the dramatic way in which the natural sounds and scents of the outside were replaced by others. The doors leading from the vestibule into the Hall were open, and as the green-baize door at the far end of the Hall swung open and shut, familiar sounds and scents flooded in: the clatter of the *batterie de cuisine* and the aroma of a variety of mushroom that grew wild on Møn.

'Bring me all the berries for the *rødgrød!*' a woman's voice called out in Danish.

'Coming!' a younger voice replied cheerfully.

Danish! That extraordinary language! Not beautiful in itself but made beautiful by the countless expressions of compassion it had conveyed.

'I have prepared your usual room,' Fru Møller advised, as she sat down at her desk and noted her guest's arrival in the reservations book. 'The yellow room, sea-facing.'

Miss Danziger followed Bertha upstairs, but whereas the young woman strode purposefully, she climbed slowly and paused on each landing to look down, over the banisters, into the Hall. By the time she reached the bedroom Bertha had already thrown open the windows onto the narrow balcony. 'It's been such a lovely day! What a pity you've had to spend it in trains and buses!' She set down the suitcase on the luggage rack.

Miss Danziger wandered to the window; draughts of sea air were being wafted in on a light breeze, caught in the billowing muslin curtains. As she filled her lungs she noticed the air was moist, scented with seaweed. The sound of a lawn-mower was just audible. And as she strained to enjoy the sounds of labour in which she was not involved, Elisabeth Danziger caught the 'ping' of tennis balls being whacked by racquets. A few puffs of white cloud drifted across the sky. The sun bleached the gravel on the terrace. The blood-red geraniums rolled their heads against the sides of their tumbrels. Miss Danziger was tired; it had been a long day. And she was hungry; she had not eaten on the train from Esbjerg to Copenhagen. Bertha slipped in unnoticed and left a tray.

When eventually Miss Danziger turned from her reflections and saw the tray, she took it and set it down on the balcony table. Bertha had brought her an open sandwich of rye bread on which were arranged slices of rare beef in a fan pattern garnished with grated horseradish and *rémoulade* sauce; and to drink, a tall Holmgaard tumbler of iced beer. There was a slice of *abelsnitter* and a vacuum flask of black coffee with a jug of cream and a small bowl of sugar lumps.

The white tray had a border of cerulean blue, the crockery was white with a pattern of cornflowers and the napkin cerulean, also. The cleanliness, the attention to detail, the stylishness of the simple preparation filled Miss Danziger with melancholy.

It took almost no time for her to unpack her case. She arranged her writing paper and envelopes and copy of *Mansfield Park* on the bedside table. She removed her bottle of eau-de-Cologne from her sponge bag and placed it alongside her book. She would need only one drawer of the oak chest of drawers for her belongings, but opened all five for the sheer pleasure of seeing the fresh lining paper. She hung two cotton blouses in the wardrobe on hangers to which lavender bags had been attached, and before closing the wardrobe doors pressed the bags between her fingers and inhaled the scent. From the oak book trough on the chest of drawers Miss Danziger drew two volumes: *Marie Grubbe* by J. P. Jacobsen and *A Guide to the Burial Mounds on Møn*. She removed her skirt and her blouse and kicked off her shoes. She settled herself on the bed and opened the *Guide*:

The want of a work on the barrows of Møn like the present one has long been acknowledged as a particular desideratum in this country. After the most mature consideration and a frequent and careful contemplation of the subject, I have deemed it my pleasurable duty to supply this. I am confident that in detaining you, reader, for no more than one hundred pages, I shall transform you into friend.

Smiling, she sought the date of publication, 1847, and closing the *Guide* took up *Marie Grubbe*. Rifling through the pages she stopped and read at the point where Marie, having been unhappy as a rich woman of the idle classes, extols her present life. Now more than sixty years of age, she rows the ferry while her poverty-stricken husband drinks what little he makes.

When Miss Danziger awoke from her light slumbers Marie Grubbe was on her mind: she had been dreaming of her, as a girl, at Tjele. She was wrested back into the present by the sound of the tennis players returning to bath and change for dinner; she heard feet crunch up the gravel and voices talking languidly. As feet and voices entered the house, and their sounds faded, she noticed that the hum of the lawn-mower had ceased. She could hear the sea breathing through the twittering of the sparrows that nested in the wisteria. She consulted her watch; she rose, put a cotton kimono over her petticoat, threw a salt-white bath towel over her arm, picked up her sponge bag, opened the bedroom door quietly, looked right and left along the corridor and, satisfied that no one was about, crossed quickly to the bathroom.

The bathroom had been newly painted; the walls were shining, glossy white. But it preserved all its Edwardian fittings – a polished wood-plank floor, a huge tub garnished with nine-inch brass taps and a brass plunging mechanism that did service for a plug. There was the freestanding, square wash-basin with a stem of convolvulus running from the pedestal into the bowl, and there the mahogany-framed looking-glass above the basin. There, too, the mahogany panels with their polished ornamental brass screws! Miss Danziger was consoled: everything was just the same as ever it had been. She turned on the bath taps. She zipped open her sponge bag and took from it a screwdriver. As noiselessly as she was able, she unscrewed one of the panels round the tub, confident that the sound of the running water would mask any noise her activities might create. Having detached the panel she laid it gently on the bath mat and thrust her arm up to the elbow under the bath. From the subterranean depths she retrieved a small box. She blew away the dust that lay on the surface of the box before sitting down on the cane-seated chair and lifting the lid. Inside the box a tiny ammonite lay on a bed of yellowing cotton wool. Reading from a crumbling piece of lined paper Miss Danziger intoned in a whisper, 'Daniel Eberhardt/Elisabeth Danziger, nineteen thirty.'

The gong sounded. Entering the dining-room on the first evening of her annual holiday was always a particular trial for Elisabeth. For many years she had had only two ways of tackling it to preserve her anonymity: either to enter early and be seated by the time the other guests arrived, so that she did not have to walk to her table alone, under the gaze of up to eighteen pairs of eyes, or to slip in late, when everyone was preoccupied in choosing from an assortment of soups and hors d'œuvres. More recently she had discovered a third alternative: to descend the stairs in the company of one or two other guests, exchanging small talk. Her very proximity to them rendered her inconspicuous. After having said good-evening, and asking her whether she had had a good day, the guest would speak of his or her own interests, inevitably overlooking Elisabeth, with her unfashionable hair-style, her faded dress, and above all her status as an *habituée*. As for eating alone, she welcomed it. Not only was she accustomed to it but, because she had a tendency to choke on her food, she was obliged to concentrate on her chewing and permit only a small, soft gobbet to proceed down her throat at one gulp. It made her less anxious if she was able to give these precautions her undivided attention.

Fru Møller's courtesy, indisputable though it was, lacked feeling. Better by far to have accomplished its semblance than not, in her business; nevertheless it was of a variety not altogether consoling to those who had rumbled its purpose. Miss Danziger had done so years ago. Although Fru Møller always reserved Miss Danziger a table overlooking the terrace, and was careful to leave a decent path between tables for her to reach it, she was not so careful to talk to her guests in a low voice, and so Miss Danziger's regular return to The Tamarisks all too quickly became common knowledge, and so too did her daily excursions.

'So regular in her habits!' Fru Møller would exclaim to any guest within earshot. 'She's been coming to us for fifteen years, arriving on the Sunday and leaving on the following Sunday, and I can guarantee to forecast precisely where she will be on the island at any moment of her stay!'

In the early post-war days Fru Møller had hoped that Miss Danziger might blaze a trail that would lead a file of English tourists to The Tamarisks. With this expectation in mind, on the only occasion Miss Danziger requested her discretion, Fru Møller not only gave it unhesitatingly but subsequently adhered to it unfailingly: she should not mention, ever, that Miss Danziger was connected with The Tamarisks and had known Møn before the war. That was all. And Miss Danziger would not wish to discuss further with Fru Møller her connection with the house.

When young Ilsa Torve left school she went into domestic service. Although excellent in the performance of her duties, she had not been fortunate in her employer. She left as soon as she was able to do so without fear of forfeiting an excellent reference and went into the Danish Tourist Offices in Copenhagen as a clerk. There she made friends with Sussi Blicher, also a young clerk, also from the provinces, and met and married the publicity officer, Jens Møller. On the sudden, unexpected death of Jens at the age of thirty, a 'new broom' was acquired. It was he who initiated the idea of Ilsa Møller and Sussi Blicher running the two houses on Møn as exclusive guest-houses. At the time, Møn did not feature on the tourist map. A few families from Copenhagen, Odense and Aarhus had country cottages on the island but the Germans who, during the Health and Beauty craze of the twenties and thirties, had enjoyed nude bathing under the celebrated white cliffs of Møn, were not yet confident of the warm reception their holiday breaks demanded, and had not trickled back. No foreign tourists from elsewhere materialised. The question the Tourist Board asked itself was: what sort of tourists do we want? On consulting the residents of Møn they were told, 'Rare ones.' The Tourist Board took their point.

Between them the Tuscan Villa and The Tamarisks could comfortably accommodate about forty visitors at a time. The Villa, with its unrivalled collection of early musical instruments, was designed to attract those wanting the opportunity to try out medieval instruments that they would otherwise never be permitted so much as to hold. The Tamarisks, with its unparalleled collection of English *objets d'art*, would it was hoped attract Anglophiles from within Denmark itself, together with visitors from England interested in their country's cultural influence on an island, not previously known to them, belonging to a country they had never colonised. For, although it had been a German who had revived the English connection, the museum on Møn provided evidence of such a connection dating back to much earlier times.

'May I?' and before Miss Danziger was able to gather her forces to murmur 'please do', and swallow the last mouthful of *kransekager* (a slice of which wedding cake Bertha's mother, the cook at The Tamarisks, had put by for her), Fru Møller had drawn up a chair and sat down at Miss Danziger's table. Fru Møller's expertise was nowhere more striking than in the dining-room. She succeeded in exercising complete control over the smooth running of mealtimes without appearing to be more than a vague presence in the Hall. She liked to take her guests' orders herself; she never wrote down anything and she never forgot anything. And she only intervened where she knew her gesture would be welcome – a matter regarding which her instinct was unerring. At the end of dinner she gently persuaded her guests into the study, where she presided over the Cona coffee machine and orchestrated conversation between strangers.

Miss Danziger was obliged to pay the price for having put Fru Møller at a disadvantage early in their relationship; the price incurred was a little more intimacy than she would have chosen – and certainly more than Fru Møller exacted from her other guests. On this particular evening, as the visitors trailed off in the direction of coffee, Fru Møller, knowing to a split second how long the Cona would take to prepare its aromatic brew, spent the intervening minutes reciting to Miss Danziger the latter's inevitable itinerary for the morrow.

'Tomorrow' (*Und morgen wird die Sonne wieder scheinen* . . .), 'we're promised fine weather, Miss Danziger. You'll be glad of the sun at Liselund!' And, on receiving neither confirmation nor contradiction, Fru Møller quickly continued, 'I always tell my guests: ours is not the first experiment with culture in the wilderness. Go to Liselund! See for yourselves!'

'Have this week's been?'

'Indeed they have! I managed to pack them off last Wednesday!' Fru Møller confirmed with pride. Miss Danziger was relieved. She would probably have both the house and the park to herself. Tomorrow.

Fru Møller could not cope with silences, they made her nervous. The one that ensued she endeavoured to fill by picking up Miss Danziger's empty pudding plate and holding it at arm's length so that Bertha, who was clearing the tables, would see her gesture and be obliged to relieve her of the plate. More than likely, Bertha would attempt to prise a few words from Fru Møller's taciturn guest.

'Did you enjoy the *kransekager*? Mother made it for my friend's wedding last week. She remembered it was a favourite of yours.' Bertha stood looking at Miss Danziger. She appraised her frankly. 'You're looking so well!' she said warmly. 'But even when you arrive with the big city all

34

about you, it never takes long for you to look happy and countrified like us.' Bertha was gifted in creating well-being. She had known Miss Danziger since she was a child. She liked the older woman. She willed her tranquillity.

Fru Møller was grateful to Bertha for her few words but did not allow control of the conversation to be wrested from her. She rose from her chair and, with an eloquent sniff and mere twitch of her nostrils, lowered her head and confided, 'The Colonel and his lady arrive tomorrow. I need not tell you how little the prospect of their Boo-Boo/Bo-Bo talk attracts me.' By showing her intolerance of the Colonel and his wife, Fru Møller was departing from her customary discretion. She did so not only because she wished to make clear her contempt for a couple willing to make a display of their intimacies, but also as a means of showing Elisabeth Danziger what she felt about the latter's relationship with the Colonel.

Having succinctly made her points, Fru Møller deftly turned the conversation elsewhere, taking Elisabeth with her. 'I imagine you've spotted Mitzi Baum? I must say, I never expected her to book with us again.' Fru Møller's voice dropped a few tones lower, into the key of confidentiality. 'You remember how after five consecutive years she suddenly missed three? It was the Colonel, of course. He said something unfortunate.' Fru Møller was nodding her head. Elisabeth was reminded of an advertisement in her local chemist's with a small bird dipping its head up and down into a bowl of water – was it to demonstrate perpetual motion, she was wondering. 'You do remember, Miss Danziger?'

35

'Yes.' And she had noticed Mitzi at dinner. The woman had been allotted the least well-positioned table, by the green-baize door. Had there been a cloakroom giving off the Hall Fru Møller would no doubt have placed Mitzi to its side. Nothing about Mitzi appeared to have changed during the intervening years; she was dressed, as usual, in her Austrian peasant costume. Perhaps she had put on a little weight . . . the costume seemed stretched almost beyond endurance across her excessive bosom and buttocks. Mitzi must be sixty, Elisabeth calculated. She was a spinster. The reason for her unmarried status was common knowledge; she liked to talk about it.

The man marked out for Mitzi Baum by her parents, when she was but a slip of a thing, had failed to produce an engagement ring of the size and quality required by the family. Fräulein Baum had kicked her heels for two years waiting for her fellow librarian to deliver, miraculously, a suitably cut, weighty brilliant and, with his failure to do so, had given him his marching orders, since when no suitable man had shown interest in the Fräulein's hand. The Colonel, in an effort to be chivalrous, had succeeded in upsetting Mitzi Baum by suggesting over coffee one evening, in a stage whisper that could be heard clearly by the assembled company, that he was in no doubt subsequent suitors had shown plenty of interest in other regions of her body. Mitzi Baum was at first flattered by this suggestion, but on weighing up the Colonel's clumsy attempt at humour, she had found it to contain the implication that no other man had wished to explore her mind, or had thought her good enough for him. So she concluded that she was offended.

She had tried to make a friend of the Colonel by confiding in him. He had taken advantage of her!

Miss Danziger, who had learnt over the years how to handle the Colonel, made it her business to pour oil on the waters he troubled. So she was obliged to give Fräulein Baum time in which to off-load her favourite topic of conversation: man's inhumanity to woman. It was not easy to imagine Mitzi Baum's nights of hectic passion between her embroidered linen sheets, but it was just these that she liked to rehearse and set against the wholly inadequate *thé dansant* and box of three Swiss handkerchiefs (machine embroidered) that her suitors offered in exchange. She had been raised, she explained, to expect financial security as evidence of a man's gratitude for her physical presence. If she was going to have to put up with him at breakfast every morning for the rest of her life, she would expect him to make it worth her while. Mitzi Baum did not demand Miss Danziger's acquiescence – only her attention. And this she received.

'Miss Danziger's a thoroughly good sort!' Fräulein Baum said of her behind her back. To her face she assumed an expression as near that of tenderness as she was able to approach, confident that unmarried women are all sisters under the skin.

'I just knew you'd understand, my dear!' she said, in no way anxious as to how Miss Danziger would interpret her experience.

Elisabeth climbed the stairs wearily, closing the ante-chamber of her mind against all thoughts of the past that had gathered there and pressed for an audience. Her bedroom had lost its singularity – once hers, today anyone's – yet the furniture and fittings were the same. The bed, once a dreamer's now more like a patient's; the table – devoid of notebooks, music scores, photographs, pressed flowers, fossils – coldly austere. Meaningless. The upright chair slipped under the table reminiscent of the schoolroom. She turned off the light and went to stand on the balcony. Night had crept onto the terrace below and the sea heaved peacefully.

MONDAY

It was deliciously cool cycling through the green shade of the forest. Elisabeth noticed just how cool when she emerged on to the cliff path and into the full glare of the sun. For three kilometres she would need to follow the contours of the luminous chalk cliffs that plunged 130 metres to the pebbled shore. She kept her eyes fastened to the path as she pedalled ahead. Recognising a patch of long grass on her left, she drew off the path sharply and let her cycle fall to the ground. And then she walked back to the path, dropped to her knees on the narrow grass verge and crawled to the edge of the cliffs on her stomach. She forced herself to peer over the edge; she was terrified of heights these days. Down where the sea met the sand, beyond the pebbles, little waves were curling timidly; waters from the incoming tide had sought out and collected in rock pools to sulk until the outgoing tide came to gather them in and return them to their source. Far out at sea, where ultramarine turned to Prussian, three fishing boats floated motionless.

The day was simmering. A few gulls drifted over the sea as if wasting time. Elisabeth dragged her cycle out of the long grass, mounted and turned inland. A pattern of old lace spread itself over the velvety ground where the sun filtered through the leaves of the beech trees. Butterflies, enjoying their boundless carnality, flitted in the sunbeams.

It was evident at a distance of a hundred metres where the nave of trees through which she was riding came to an end and the path emerged on exposed land. A gentle grassy hill sloped down to the house. At the summit of the hill a bench was sited; it had its back to the beeches and faced over the lake and the grotto on to the house. Elisabeth sat down and focused her attention on Liselund. Her right hand had sought the arm of the bench and was folding itself round the warm, smooth wood. Her impatient fingers were feeling up and down the underside of the arm. Her action was imperceptible and involuntary; had she been in company no one would have noticed that her concentration was divided between the view of the lake and house she faced and the arm of the bench under her fingers. Satisfied she was alone she dropped to her knees and peered under the arm. She found what she sought: an 'E' and a 'D' and a date, 1933, followed by the words *à l'amitié pure.*

Liselund was built by Antoine Bosc de la Calmette in 1792 for his twenty-year-old mistress who would later become his wife. Calmette was an enthusiastic follower of Jean-Jacques Rousseau and Liselund has been called a Baltic Petit Trianon. Its exterior is whitewashed brick and it has a thatched roof. Its interior extends to a few sparsely furnished, coolly elegant rooms with long windows providing light, and mirrors from floor to ceiling providing an illusion of space. As he intended the building to be a summer retreat, Calmette was at pains to ensure that Andreas Kirkerup, the distinguished architect, restrained himself and did not give way to his classical predilections.

Liselund is set in a park between a hill, a lake and the sea. There are ancient beech trees overlooking the house on high ground, and in the middle ground a lake, numerous fountains, lovingly tended flower-beds and rare shrub enclosures. Peacocks wander the park, trailing enamelled tails, their shrill voices raised in marked contrast to their elegant gait. Here at Liselund, Calmette created culture in the wilderness.

Among monuments in the garden may be found, in Mme Lise's favourite spot, a stone pillar with a marble relief showing two of the three Graces, with the gallant husband's inscription, *Elles attendent icy Leur sœur*. In a grotto facing the Swiss House, one of the three garden houses, the portrait of Lise may be seen incised on a medallion, surrounded by the dedication: *à l'amitié pure*.

As she walked downhill Elisabeth found the guidebook litany repeating itself in her head.

Liselund was shut; according to a handwritten notice, pinned on the door, the guide would open the house at 2 p.m. Elisabeth walked round the house, peering through the windows. On her first tour she concentrated her attention on the white and green painted furniture and the silk drapes, on her second on the tented bed and the ox-blood red walls, and on her third on the monkey painted on the central panel of the looking-glass, flanked by beautifully modelled palm-tree trunks. The court decorator had been given a free hand with landscapes and had chosen to celebrate the pet monkey of an ancestor of Calmette, which had saved its owner's life by waking him when his house caught fire. But the rooms struck Elisabeth as desolate – like a stage when the play is over, the lights turned off and the players gone home.

The Swiss House, used as a refreshment kiosk, was also shut and would reopen only when the house reopened. Elisabeth sat at a table in the tiny forecourt. Her still scrutiny of the lake attracted a peacock. The bird walked towards her and then round her, several times, as if intent upon casting a spell on an intruder. Then it howled like a damned soul. Elisabeth felt her present self wane; she was on the brink of dissolution. Against her inclination, and in spite of her determination, forces stronger than her consciousness lured her deeper and deeper back, down, into the past.

❖

'Good-evening! My name is Elisabeth Danziger. I don't think we've met before.' No, they had not. They had not been on Møn before. Their name: Hulsby. They came from Odense.

'Is there anything to do on Møn? We came for a rest but we hate to be idle.'

'Well, there's lots to see!' Miss Danziger was relieved to find herself at the entrance to the Hall by the time this conversation had yielded all it possibly might. The newcomers were ushered by Fru Møller to a table by the window. Elisabeth sidled to her own. But why, oh why, had Fru Møller seated the Colonel and his wife so near to her this year? She was going to overhear their conversation however hard she strained to avoid listening to it.

'Boo-Boo, what shall I take as an hors d'œuvre?'

'Bo-Bo always enjoys the cheese puffs . . . '

'Do I? I forget . . . '

When he saw Miss Danziger enter, the Colonel raised his backside two inches from his chair. The gesture was almost imperceptible, but peculiarly eloquent: he was not going to ignore Elisabeth, nor was he going to upset Bo-Bo. He was not going to forfeit his command of good manners, nor was he going to display them ostentatiously.

Colonel Jensen was sixty-five years of age. His wife was nearer seventy; she had lied so often about the date of her birth that for many years she had been genuinely unsure of it herself. The Colonel, on the other hand, was punctilious with fact – a quality appreciated in the regular army from which he had retired a year ago. It was his marriage that had been responsible for his not being accorded the advancement to which his capabilities had entitled him. He knew this and took it in his stride. He was as fastidious over his personal appearance as he was with matters of fact. He had once seen Kokoschka's portrait of Joseph de Montesquiou Fezensac, noticed how closely he resembled the sitter, obtained a reproduction of the portrait and from that day modelled himself on the man. Like his model he was thin, had a receding hairline, bright blue eyes shaded by a protruding brow, a well-proportioned nose and, to perfect the resemblance, he had grown a light moustache. He favoured high collars and knotted cravats and, when out

walking, was inseparable from one or other of his meticu-
lously selected walking canes.

Colonel Jensen returned annually to Møn in pursuit of
his passion for moths and fossils. He owed his interests to
his father, who had encouraged in the boy pursuits that
did not depend upon company, for the family lived at the
extreme north of Jutland, remote from even the small
village where they sold their catch. As the Colonel became
increasingly isolated – on account of the bizarre behaviour
of his wife – he found it more palatable to return to a guest-
house where he and his wife were known, and explanations
were not invited.

Bo-Bo, on whose birth certificate appeared the perfectly
respectable and pretty name Beatrice, was a victim of an
idyllic childhood out of which she had resolutely refused
to emerge. She had been a pretty child easily adored, and
she had grown into a beautiful young woman whose sole
ambition was to be admired. She went on the stage; there
she was suitably cast in *ingénue* roles and encouraged to
re-enact her childhood.

It was love at first sight for the Colonel – a lieutenant at
the time. He sat in the stalls night after night until he plucked
up the required courage to join the queue of admirers that
waited for Beatrice at the stage door. He wooed her with
arum lilies, French scent and illustrated children's books –
replicas of ones her parents had disposed of from her shelves
when she left home at seventeen.

It had been plain sailing from the moment the young
man had understood that he would be best appreciated
playing the role of generous father to her pert, pretty,

everlastingly young daughter. Being profoundly puritanical (Lutheranism had been a mighty force in north Jutland), the Lieutenant expected there would be a high price to pay for his lust. He might not have calculated that the payments would continue throughout his life, but on discovering that this was the case, he behaved impeccably.

'Is your lady friend here?' pouted Fru Jensen.

'Yes. Miss Danziger's here. Of course she is! She never misses!'

'I shall show her baby-doll!' And the Colonel's wife took up her napkin and dabbed the corners of her mouth.

When she was not knitting – mostly for herself in her preferred tones of rose, auburn, cherry and peach – Fru Jensen sewed clothes for her many dolls. She smocked, she appliquéd, she embroidered; and she strove to detain anyone willing to inspect her handicraft. Once detained, her audience might be captivated by her work and stay to admire longer than they had anticipated. Thus the Colonel's lady sometimes won for herself attention that was appreciative. Ordinarily, she was the object of amusement – even ridicule. And if she was unaware of that, she was aware of her isolation. The Colonel had long since abandoned any attempt to influence his wife's manner of expression or her conversation, which revolved round the triality of food, dress and dolls. Bo-Bo was peculiarly fascinated by all that could be ingested. She was equally attracted by fish, fowl, meat and the vegetable kingdom, and with all the fervour of an ancient Greek storyteller would trace their metamorphoses – that of a radish from a seed into a rose, garnishing an open sandwich; that of a trout from an egg in a stream into a grilled fish, speckled with toasted almonds, on a silver platter; that of a wild deer into a haunch of venison, accompanied by currant jelly the fruit of which the animal itself might have enjoyed when it was on the hoof.

Similarly, with clothes: she not only observed keenly what was available in the shops but imagined how every garment might be improved upon. 'Had the lace been Brussels and the tiny stitching picked out in emerald and not that dull sepia, the effect might have been charming . . . ' Yet she herself dressed in the manner of an only child of eight, and dyed her hair pink to match her assortment of frocks, cardigans and shoes.

'You can show her over coffee.'

'And to tell the truth . . . ' Bo-Bo started.

'*Toute vérité n'est pas bonne à dire*, my dear,' the Colonel interrupted, knowing where his wife's line of conversation was leading. She was lifting the doll's skirts, exposing its knickers. Shortly, she would confide in a stage whisper to Miss Danziger that this doll had a tendency to soil her underwear and required frequent changing.

The seeming neglect that was a feature of the study was only temporary and was designed: Fru Møller imagined her guests felt more relaxed, when they had finished a meal, in an atmosphere of careful disarray. She accomplished this by strewing the magazines, papers and guidebooks over the tables and chairs and ostentatiously gathering them up as her guests assembled for after-dinner coffee. 'Strew' was a word Fru Møller savoured for its suggestion of chaos, a state of affairs with which she was not familiar, which stood well outside her domain, and which appeared dangerously attractive and more redolent of Copenhagen than Møn. So long as she could be in charge of chaos she could entertain it. She would not, however, keep a dog or a cat.

When Bo-Bo entered the study – followed closely by her husband – Fru Møller was in the act of making a neat pile of magazines and placing them on the window-seat.

'I know my guests! You'd all rather be outdoors than stuck inside reading! I just keep these for our rare rainy days!'

Bo-Bo, however, was not addicted to the outside. She collected several magazines and examined pictures of a baby-pink bedjacket and a peach-sequined evening wrap, before contentedly immersing herself in useful tips on personal hygiene, wreaths of dried flowers and painless childbirth.

Bo-Bo had but two expressions: one of sorrow and one of pleasure. She alternated between the two as she read. The expression of sorrow indicated that she was absorbed by the fiction sections. These were ample and confined them-selves to tales of unrequited love. A look of pleasure took the place of sorrow when Bo-Bo turned to a pattern for a knitted mitten or a recipe for herring salad. There was no prior warning of her return to speech.

'Look who it is who's smuggled herself into my pocket!' At the unheralded blast the assembled company risked spilling their coffee over themselves and their neighbours. It would have been impossible to fathom the link between what Bo-Bo was reading and what led her to fumble in her pocket. She let her magazine drop to the floor. Eight quiet guests, some talking in low voices, others leafing through magazines that did not interest them, shook themselves free from their forays into the unknown, the fantastic and the boring to be greeted by Bo-Bo holding aloft a four-inch person kitted out in Icelandic costume. The interruption served to intensify the guests' determination to read. They were frustrated in this, for Bo-Bo's reading was fitful, punctuated by talk that lurched from one triviality to another and only righted itself in the moments of silence when she returned to an absorbing knitting pattern or recipe. In those rare periods, regarded by the Colonel and other guests as beyond compare, the sound of Bo-Bo sucking boiled sweets and rattling them between her teeth seemed dauntingly loud.

Miss Danziger, in an effort to gather together the shattered elements of a tranquil evening, allowed herself to be hijacked by Bo-Bo who untiringly introduced her to a basketful of dolls. She led Bo-Bo into the vestibule, sat with her on the floor and listened as the old woman let herself be drawn back in the slipstream of time to her ecstatic infancy.

'Thank you for showing me your lovely family and your beautiful work,' Elisabeth said, rising from the floor only when she felt she decently might. 'I think I shall wander down to the shore and get a glimpse of the sea before I turn in.' The Colonel emerged from the study and she saw him move towards the front door in anticipation of accompanying her. She gave him a barely perceptible shake of her head that he fully understood.

'*Und auf dem Wege* . . . ' Elisabeth hummed in her head as she walked across the terrace. Lights from the Hall cast rectangular shapes on the ground. Voices in the study were just audible, discussing tomorrow's fishing expedition: 'Tomorrow . . . ' The clink of glass and the deeper tone made by a cup on a saucer meant that schnapps was being served with more coffee.

The Tamarisk Path was left lighted until all the guests had gone to bed so that anyone wishing for a breath of sea air last thing would not risk stumbling in the dunes. The air was heavy; a storm threatened, but for the time being the sea was in a friendly mood. Small waves chuckled before giving little sighs of pleasure as the waters moved gently back and forth, teasing the shingle.

As she passed the open study door on her way upstairs, Elisabeth heard Bo-Bo's voice rise high above that of the other guests: 'This one's called Daisy because she's so fresh. And this one's called Ivy, she's so grown round my heart.'

TUESDAY

Elisabeth woke early; it was still dark and she could hear that the wind was up, threatening the air, poised to burst into uncontrollable rage. She rose, pulled her kimono over her shoulders, and approached the window. Over a barely discernible grey sheet of water was thrown an equally grey shroud of sky, but the shroud was torn in places to reveal streaks of blood red and aquamarine blue. Elisabeth opened the window and stepped out onto the balcony. She watched as the jagged tears in the sky mended, cobbling themselves together in a uniform grey. Drops of heavy rain pelted the balcony with silver stones. The sorrow of the sky was dissolving; under it the relentless heaving of the compassionless waters mocked the sky's concern. And then the sky itself raged. A sheet of lightning flashed across the waters, to be followed, seconds later, by a roll of thunder. The grey ocean seethed. Above and beneath an endless expanse of heavy, undulating danger was let loose.

'That poor dear woman!' Fru Gertlinger, Bertha's mother, was on the verge of tears. 'And she doesn't come from a fishing family herself. Her folk farmed. She's got four little ones.' Certain that none of the men on the *Flounder* would have survived, she named each of them. She knew them all; she was devastated for them and their families, who would be left husbandless and fatherless. But it was over the husband of her closest friend that she grieved most deeply. 'I hate the sea! Even before it took Peter from me, I hated the sea. It is insatiable.'

Guests ate breakfast in silence as the rain poured monotonously out of the grey sky and thudded on the roof, the balconies and the terrace. They were resentful. Rain on holiday – so much wetter, somehow, than rain at other times. What was there to do on Møn in the rain? Plans once agreed could be unmade, at a practical level, but somehow, and on some other level, what had been planned remained a possibility and hung around to haunt them. What they had wanted was to have gone on a fishing expedition. Such a delightful prospect! And now this had happened! It might blight the whole of their stay . . .

'I'm sure of one thing,' Fru Møller said darkly, to no one in particular, as she left the Hall to collect raspberry jam from the kitchen for a guest allergic to strawberries, 'the rain won't deflect Miss Danziger from her purpose.' From behind the door that swung closed against her back, the guests heard Fru Møller tell Fru Gertlinger to put more coffee on to brew: 'They'll be sitting about all morning in weather like this!'

'Miss Danziger likes to keep to a routine, whatever the obstacles, don't you, Miss Danziger?' Fru Møller continued, as she re-entered the Hall. 'And she likes the house to stay just the same,' she remarked to Fru Gertlinger, as she swept back through the green-baize door for yet more toast, 'so she's not going to object to the blue room being returned to its former colours. Did I mention, I discovered a dozen rolls of the original wallpaper in a tin trunk in the attic? I think it's going to be usable; it doesn't seem to have dried out.'

Back and forth Fru Møller passed from the Hall to the kitchen, replenishing the bread-baskets, the toast-racks, the milk jugs and cream pots, enquiring, 'Fräulein Baum, may I offer you a soft-boiled egg?'

'That would be nice, Fru Møller. And d'you know what? I think I could manage two!'

'Does it always rain on Møn in August?' Fru Hulsby tentatively enquired.

Fru Møller, loyal to her country in general and her corner of it particularly, assured the newcomer that in living memory it had hardly ever done so. 'This is most unusual!'

'Boo-Boo! Listen to me, Boo-Boo!' The Colonel emerged from behind his newspaper to allow his wife a view of his expressionless face. Her plaintive whisper had projected itself right round the Hall, but this had not put paid to her determination to secure his attention. 'Fru Møller just told that lady that it never rains here in August, but the dolls say it often does and they packed their mackintoshes!'

❖

When the Tuscan Villa and The Tamarisks came to the notice of the Tourist Board and before either was converted into a guest-house, the road that served The Tamarisks and then swung inland, downhill, to the rear of the Tuscan Villa, was extended. It was impossible to extend it to the front of the

Villa without blasting the cliffs and destroying exquisite country, but quite possible to reach the gates at the rear of the park. But it was not the new road that Miss Danziger took in the rain that morning. She followed the old route, through the walled garden at The Tamarisks to the path that curled down the cliffs to the five-acre plateau on which the Villa stood at the centre of an arboretum.

Some of the rare trees planted by the original owner of the Tuscan Villa had been replaced. Most, however, had reached and even overshot their maturity; they had become the elder statesmen of their breeds: exceptional, memorable examples of the extremes nature is capable of attaining. Here, trees broke all records for their height, the width of their branch span and the luxuriousness of their foliage. Despite the proximity of the sea and the mean wind that gathered and spread salt, this community of trees was renowned for its health. Botanists suggested that by some felicitous intuition the Italian planter had chosen specimens with properties that facilitated each other's growth. Møn was filled with such examples of co-operation, they said.

The arboretum was known simply as the Park, and was open to the public. However, the public on Møn was a small one and the Park was visited primarily by public servants from other parts of Denmark, whose job it was to plant out public places – and also by visitors to the Villa and The Tamarisks. In the rain, Elisabeth was alone – apart from the sheep lent to crop the grass.

She was filled with an overwhelming sense of loss as she wandered from tree to tree, recognising many, feeling

54

herself accused: she had overstayed her welcome in the world. Life conducted itself independently of her. The scents from the sodden earth filled her with an intolerable weight of memory; not that of individual occasions but of the entire past.

She approached the catalpa tree. The expanded E and D would have been invisible to anyone not expecting to find them. As she drew her finger along the initials, her stomach clenched and her eyes misted. She beat on the tree with her fists, she threw her arms as far round the tree as they would reach and then, despite the relentless rain, the saturated ground and the penetrating cold, she fell on her knees at its foot, unable to muster the will to walk on.

It was an old ewe, treading on the skirt of her raincoat, that roused Elisabeth. Slowly she dragged herself along one of the paths that led to the house. But she did not approach the house. She sheltered in a summer-house twenty metres from the windows of the music room.

The moist silence was being broken by birdsong; it was a hectic chattering, insistent, like the rain. No one was about. The windows of the Villa were firmly shut. Garden furniture had been neatly stacked under the colonnade. Elisabeth was torn between retreating at once, following the path back the way she had come, or continuing as far as the colonnade to look through the windows into the music room. Her indecision made her sweat; her armpits felt clammy under her raincoat and the palms of her hands were moist. Why should she feel like this: as if she were engaged in something illegal? This was a public park. Now. She was entitled to be here. No notice suggested that visitors were trespassers. Yet, she felt, it was not done to peer. How, she wondered, might she look in without seeming nosy? And what was it she wanted to see, precisely? Unable to answer her own questions, she turned back without approaching the Villa. It was still there! That was what mattered. And the Park was being beautifully maintained; the trees were not being needlessly felled; the formal garden that girdled the house retained all its statuary . . .

It was midday by the time Miss Danziger walked through the entrance of The Tamarisks. The rain had stopped. She would change out of her wet clothes before going into Gullshaven to the museum, she decided.

'Svend Larsen rang! It can't be more than three minutes ago. He was wanting to know whether he could expect you for lunch.' Fru Møller was at her desk, 'on the bridge', as she expressed it.

'He knows I always visit the museum on Tuesday.'

'Well, Miss Danziger, you must allow it is rather unusual for guests to keep engagements from one *year* to the next, as you do. Shall I telephone him back and confirm?'

'I would be most obliged if you would be so kind. Tell him I'm planning to catch the 12.30 from Lakeside.'

It is impossible on Møn to be far from the sight and sound of lapping water. Miss Danziger waited at the place known as Lakeside at St Lund, where small craft poached alongside the road. There was no bus-stop as such; there was no need: everyone in the area knew this was the place at which public transport put down and picked up. Just as the bus appeared on the horizon, a peasant woman emerged, seemingly from thin air.

'Would you make a small detour for me?' she asked the driver.

'How small?' he enquired and, on being told, agreed.

The detour was to Holmstroyd and involved stopping at the jetty. From here the hull of the fishermen's boat, lashed by the high seas the previous day, could be seen ditched on a group of rocks to one side of the tiny bay. The hull was unrecognisable as such; half out of water it became unidentifiable debris. The waves that had deposited the hull and broken masts had carried with them a body – that of the only widower on board. News of this discovery had travelled quickly to the wives of the seven other fishermen, and Elisabeth saw that they were already grouped together on the shore. Baltic fishermen's wives were schooled for disaster; marrying a fisherman was not to launch life on a smooth certainty. The women stood in silence, glad of each other's presence and without the need to say as much. *Und zu dem Strand* . . .

The storm had passed and done its worst; now the women gathered, dressed alike in full dark skirts and tucked-in blouses, shawls pulled over their heads – reenacting a painting by Krøyer, their eyes fixed on the sea. Elisabeth felt disorientated. Was this a picture? Was this a performance? She had witnessed this event before. Repeatedly. *Wieder, wieder* . . .

Elisabeth did not enter the museum at once, but lingered in the courtyard. She stood fingering the tresses of the willow, branches of which wept over the upturned hull of a boat, which had been dug out of the peat bog to the north of the island and was permanently on display.

'Much perishes, of course, but, happily, something always survives!'

Elisabeth had not heard Svend Larsen approach; at the sound of his voice she turned to face him. 'I'm sorry! I'm a little late. The bus made a detour. Holmstroyd. I got distracted. Those poor waiting women . . . '

'Yes. We do seem destined as an island for these tragedies. They come along all too regularly. The Baltic's an oceanic grave.' The curator urged his visitor towards the open doors of his museum: 'Come! Let's eat!'

Svend Larsen pushed a pile of papers to one side of his desk, took a platter of open sandwiches from the top of his bookcase and set it down between Elisabeth and himself. He poured iced lager from cans. 'I have so much new to show you! We had an extraordinary stroke of luck last year. Just after you left. D'you remember I showed you a manuscript – it must've been some years ago, now – purporting to be by some mariner who remembered an English cargo boat having gone down between us, here at Møn, and Malmo – during the First Schleswig War? Well, a freak maelstrom hit us last September and drove wreckage into the bay at Moltke, where a group of German amateur divers were camping. They came across a case of English pottery and porcelain on one of their sorties and were good enough to let me know about it. Look!' And Svend Larsen pulled a cup and saucer from a drawer in his desk. 'Look at this! It's Sunderland, and after about a hundred and twenty years under the sea, the lustre's still lustrous!' Elisabeth held the cup and saucer and examined its luminous pink. 'But the thing that breaks my heart', the curator continued, 'is that there were books on board and, of course, the sea's only left indecipherable leather spines . . . We'll never know even what titles were being shipped . . . Coffee?' Larsen talked enthusiastically about his small team of volunteer divers, about their finds, about his plans for the museum. It was obvious that his enthusiasm never left him time to concentrate on eating. As he ate, he opened and closed drawers, he examined papers and objects on his desk: 'I'll let you loose in the west gallery and catch you up at the door to the stockroom. I must explain my ruse for prising so much stuff – good stuff – out of the islanders.'

Elisabeth wandered between pieces of furniture and medieval sculpture retrieved from farmhouses and churches. Although Larsen more often than not returned ecclesiastic items to hallowed ground, he kept some pieces in the museum to demonstrate the shared aesthetic dimension of the past. It was something he wanted not only to preserve but somehow to revive. Elisabeth stopped to examine the contents of a case containing the paraphernalia of marriage and its consummation, represented by illuminated bonds exchanged between families, and little crowns worn by the island brides. Babies' christening robes were particularly affecting; they might have been blown together by a soft breeze, so invisible was their stitching. The swan-white robes were not the possessions of single families but of the community, and every mother whose infant wore a robe made and sewed a tiny bow to the back of the garment, so that it might be recorded how many infants had been christened in it.

Elisabeth could remember when *batterie de cuisine* actually looked like the tools of a real trade. She had seen in her young days the island women carry brass bottomless bowls on their heads to support the old churns in which they delivered milk. And she herself had urged on the flames of the drawing room fire with a goose-feather fan, like the one in the glass case. That same design of fan was in use five hundred years ago on Møn: there was one in the frescos at Sandweg . . . And there was the delivery table! Elisabeth recalled the times she had seen the midwife arrive at a peasant's cottage . . . When she was quite small she had been surprised to see the woman carrying a folded table and a Gladstone bag. Anna had explained, and it had given her the opportunity to describe details her daughter found miraculous. And still did! Elisabeth's pace slowed. She was in something of a daze. All that English china, pottery and glass! How strange that since the eighteenth century the peasants of Møn had had a taste for English ware. What a peculiar exchange it had been: herring for the table against tableware . . .

The museum was empty of visitors and crowded with objects. All these *things*! Elisabeth thought, and the thoughts tumbled about in her head in perpetual motion. Her legs brought her to a halt in front of a glass case containing a Leeds dinner-service. The creamy glaze shone as if with some inner light. The whole collection was set off by the saxe-blue Jacobean embroidery thrown over the shelves on which the pieces were carefully arranged. A neatly printed card, discreetly placed at the hem of the embroidery, told that the contents of the case had been donated by Jurgen

Danziger, in 1933. A neighbouring case, which Elisabeth took into her field of vision without moving, was devoted to three *Hispana Moresque* plates showing three different views of the synagogue at Toledo. A similar card indicated that the plates had been donated by Horst Eberhardt, in 1933. The stillness, the cool, the quiet of the building all combined to produce an effect that was overwhelming and gave rise to a feeling of expectation. Elisabeth closed her eyes. She waited. But as she waited an obstinately persistent sound filled her head, drove itself from ear to ear, settled over her eyes and seeped through to fill the whole arena of her cranium. This dreadful invasion was one with which she was familiar: something between a hum and a buzz, and terrifying for being unresponsive to any attempt to silence it. She must wait. She must wait – as she had to when pursued by the sound at night – for it to pass. Stepping back from the display cabinets, hoping to sit down on the window-seat, she made a false move and bumped into something cold. Shocked, she turned. Confused, she heard her own voice cry out: 'A mine!'

But the object was a copper schnapps still. According to the printed card it had, until quite recently, been in (illegal) service on a farm near Marienborg. The old farmer's daughter had donated it together with the notebook the farmer (and his father before him) had kept of his sales and receipts.

'Are you all right?' Svend had come quickly. 'Of course! This wasn't here last year!' He shunted the still into a corner with his foot. Taking his visitor by the arm, he walked her slowly along the corridor. 'I must explain how I've managed to accumulate all this new stuff. As you know, my intention is to have a perfect record of the island from prehistoric to present times. You see this? Colonel Jensen has given us one case of fossils and promises us more. I don't want to survive only on donations, but we just don't have the resources to buy much. These fossils, for example, don't rewrite our history but they do illustrate it usefully. The huge one over there is his, too. And he's mounted some of his moths for us . . . Look!' Elisabeth stopped to examine a stone the dimensions of a child's bicycle wheel, in which a huge ammonite was embedded. 'I'm going to enlarge both the geological room and the botanical room,' Svend continued, barely stopping to take breath. 'A botanical illus-trator who's retired here is filling in some of the gaps in our plant and tree records. But my stroke of genius – if you will allow – has been finding a way of getting the locals to bequeath us their family treasures. Obviously people don't like to part with their heirlooms – it's like parting with something of their existence, a sort of death in life. But I seem to have hit on a compromise, a way to make them feel they still have a stake in the treasure, but in addition an enhancement of their family's reputation.' And Svend Larsen thrust a catalogue into Elisabeth's hands. 'I've given a copy free to everyone who's donated something to us. You'll see: every item is illustrated and captioned with the name of the donor by its side, his or her address, and the date of presentation. This way the islanders feel that they and their family have acquired immortality. It's worked wonders!' And so saying, Svend Larsen threw open the doors of the stock-room where stacks of tea-chests, many unopened, bore witness to the success of his operation. 'I've tried to impress on people – I go round the schools and catch them young – that if they don't leave us their stuff, uncaring descendants may simply throw out a tool, plate, picture or letter, preferring to have a stainless-steel fork, a plastic plate, a multiple . . . '

The curator and his visitor ambled through a room in which traditional Danish painted furniture was ranged. 'These fifteenth-century chests with their incised shell pattern are peculiar to Møn – I've not been able to discover any on the other islands. So too is this nineteenth-century bed. You notice the design of scabious and vetch and orchids – with the insects that depend on them? Look how it's repeated on the hangings.' Elisabeth had noticed. Behind, on the whitewashed walls, her attention had been caught by coarsely painted, evocative sea- and landscapes.

'Are any of these by names I know?'

'Jarl Jacobsen – old Mother Jacobsen's father – did that.' And he pointed to a thick impasto of raging waves. 'It's the stretch of water Marie Grubbe rowed. I'm told that the day he brought it in – a good twenty years ago – he said that because his daughter was blind there was no point in its remaining in the cottage. He said he'd hung a papier mâché tray in its place so she'd not feel the absence of the picture. I've always found it rather sad that a man could produce something as evocative as this and also produce a child who could not appreciate it.'

'Are these rugs and that table from Elling, too? They're so like those in Mother Jacobsen's cottage.'

'Yes. They could have been made by the same craftsman. Will you be going to Elling on Friday?'

63

'Of course!'

Having completed a tour of the museum, Elisabeth and Svend found themselves back in Svend's office, where fresh coffee had been placed by an unseen hand. Svend pulled out a chair for his visitor. 'I know you don't care for this topic of conversation but I'm going to bring it up again, nevertheless. I'm going to beg you to reconsider . . . Will you allow me to display your pre-war researches *and* your drawings *and* your photographs? I was looking through the material again last night: it's unique! It's the first attempt to bring together all the strands of this island's life. It was an ambitious project for such young people to embark on and it worked beautifully. Because you produced it on loose pages I could exhibit it month by month as you organised it. I understand perfectly your desire for anonymity. But would you agree now, after all these years, to let me display the work if I merely credit it to ED and DE?'

'Why would you need to draw attention to the initials?'

'Partly because they appear on the individual pages – and partly because, if I don't acknowledge authorship in some way or other, I shall be inundated with enquiries. Everything else is acknowledged. But rest assured: today's public would make nothing of ED and DE, and I promise I shall give nothing further away. I would simply place a card with the initials and dates 1921–1939 alongside the material – as I've done with the other exhibits. And I'd like to place it all between the Danziger and Eberhardt donations.' Svend Larsen was being courteous but insistent. 'Do I have your permission? If so I propose to install it tonight and invite you along to see it and make suggestions before you leave.'

'I really don't know what to say. It would be churlish to refuse you. And certainly, if it enhances appreciation of Møn, it would be churlish to refuse the island. You know what my reasons have been in the past: I just don't want to provoke interest in myself. I couldn't cope with it. But I suppose you're right: the public isn't going to notice and those who know me . . . And the material certainly belongs here. Go ahead! If that's what you want for the museum. You have my permission! But I doubt that I shall come along and see it – this year. I leave on Sunday and I have my timetable. As you know, I'm not renowned for flexibility.' She had attempted a joke, but neither Svend nor she smiled. Svend thanked her warmly and talked about next year; she would see the exhibit then, and he would welcome any suggestions she had for its display. There would be a new catalogue in five years . . .

Occasionally, and this was such an occasion, Elisabeth Danziger experienced a feeling of disorientation so powerful as to render her environment totally unfamiliar. It was as if some authoritative being had decided that from that moment the names that had applied to such objects as soap, cheese, tree or book were to be exchanged for others, and all signs of delight registered by temper tantrums. She was standing at the bus station. Youths in sweaters with numbers and initials blazened on their chests lolled against bus-stops, walls and a stationary bus; a toddler sucked on an ice lolly. The sounds of Danish mingled with those of knives drawn across a plate, the screech of jays, and the buzz and hum that rose from within her and ousted her tranquillity. She knew that she must board a bus. She would concentrate on that. All else was foreign, strange, unexpected. She must get back to The Tamarisks. Her bladder was full. She might wet the seat. And were a scream to rise in her, would she manage to suppress it before it shot from her mouth? The bus ticket: it had to be bought. Did she buy it from an office somewhere? Or the bus driver?

❖

'Ah! Miss Danziger! You're back in time for tea!' Fru Møller was 'on the bridge', attending to some papers. 'Will you take it in the drawing room with our other guests?' She must not say no, must not reveal how absurd it was to 'take' tea in a 'drawing' room. Where would they be taking it to and who would be drawing? She would pretend not to have noticed Fru Møller's absurdities. She was a silly woman. The Colonel had once said, 'Fru Møller has sacrificed all *douceur de vivre* to social conformity.'

The clocks were ticking strangely fortissimo and Fru Møller didn't even notice. Was she hard of hearing? How was it that she could *tolerate* such noise? Noise: a plague. The family Hulsby – father, mother and son – were a noisy lot. At dinner they took in their soup with gusts of air and could be heard right across the Hall. But she must not mention that. She must remember on no account to go on thinking about that or she might let something slip. And she could hear them talking through the bedroom wall. Their voices sounded intimate and trusting. Was that the language of love? She had forgotten. Or was that the language of conspiracy?

66

Mitzi Edacious Baum, well into a plate of wild strawberry tarts, her gums swollen labia, her teeth prison bars. 'I've been playing patience all afternoon, Miss Danziger! And what've you been up to?' Patience! Impossible to play at that!

'Someone once said that playing patience was the nearest thing to being dead.'

'Really, Miss Danziger! Well I never; it's not like you to be offensive!'

I must get out of here or I shall say other things. It's best to be alone when the noises get this loud. A paralysing lassitude was engulfing her and she wondered how she would muster the energy to rise from her chair, walk across the drawing room, climb the stairs, remove her outer garments. Her eyelids were closing against the sheer enormity of the prospect. But she must make an attempt.

'Was that a joke, Miss Danziger?'

'I don't think so. It was an American poet who made the observation. He was a solemn man.'

Her face conveyed none of the confusion she felt. Would it be best to accept another cup of tea before trying to climb the stairs? But she must pour it herself. She must do this with very great care, not spill it or make any sort of noise. What would they do if she farted? Had anyone been looking in the direction of Miss Danziger they would have observed a faint smile gathering at the corners of her mouth and fading as quickly as it formed. It would be wonderful to let go and throw the teapot across the room, and then the milk jug and then the sugar – lump by lump – at the family Hulsby and at Mitzi. Oh dear, here come the Colonel and his lady . . . She must get out; the Colonel's lady would be

67

bound to approach her and tell her more than she wished to know.

There must be no encroachments: they must not appropriate her memories and make them theirs. Before the Colonel and his wife had helped themselves from the sideboard to cakes and sandwiches, and Fru Møller had put down a pot of tea on the table in front of them, Elisabeth Danziger had found the strength to rise and walk slowly out of the drawing room and up the stairs. She would lie down. The noises insisted upon her serving her sentence: she must allow them to sound violently fortissimo for an hour. She screwed her face tight and then let go and relaxed the muscles. She clenched her fists and then relaxed her hands. She stretched her legs from thigh to toes – and let go. She was on the rack. She took two pills from a bottle by the bed on which she had thrown herself and crushed them between the pages of *Mansfield Park*. Even then, with a full glass of water, she found it difficult to swallow the powdery pieces.

Und auf uns sinkt des Glückes stummes Schweigen . . .

Her unfortunate gaffe over tea made it impossible for Elisabeth to offer any excuse when Mitzi Baum accosted her on the stairs on the way to dinner and asked her to share her table. Elisabeth already felt herself rebuked in the presence of Fru Møller and the Colonel – over matters beyond her control – and she was not going to add to that burden of disapproval if she could avoid it; not again. Her crisis had passed, leaving her feeling exhausted and somewhat short of breath; it would not be difficult to allow Mitzi to rehearse her grievances against the male population without herself expanding on the subject, and thus let Mitzi believe that she was in agreement with her. To do so was paramount; Mitzi's social contacts were designed for the purposes of accumulating, lining up, and arming allies. But she must mind her p's and q's and be on her guard against initiating topics that she could not control. Yet the overwhelming problem was other: Elisabeth knew that there was steak on the menu for dinner.

Steak was a dish Elisabeth avoided. However, she could not avoid it at The Tamarisks, for although Fru Møller offered a generous choice of hors d'œuvres and puddings she did not provide a choice of main course and Elisabeth would not have dreamt of placing herself at a disadvantage by drawing attention to her disability and pleading for something easier than steak to swallow.

While Elisabeth concentrated unswervingly on chewing, regretting the absence of a serrated steak-knife, which would have made the cutting of the meat into very small slices so much easier, Mitzi was intent upon communication. 'I told him, I said, I have a perfectly good job, a nice home and an adequate income, what do I need with you?' Elisabeth calculated correctly that a glance in Mitzi's direction would satisfy the Austrian that she was being listened to. 'They're all the same. They imagine they're God's gift to us! So I said, frankly, all I'll get is your laundry, another cup, saucer and plate to wash up and probably a great deal more you-know-what than I need!' Lowering her voice she added confidentially, 'He was years younger than I.' Then, turning her attention to her steak, and in a tone as shocked as the one she selected to convey her distrust of the male, she asked, 'D'you know what breed of cattle they slaughter for meat?' Elisabeth did, but shook her head in order to provide Mitzi with the opportunity to inform her. 'Black and White Danish Dairy! Nothing near as tasty and tender as our . . . ' and, her mouth overflowing with steak, beans and croquette potato, Mitzi named an Austrian breed Elisabeth had never heard of (and did not imagine she would need to remember for future use). 'I like my steak burnt to a cinder on the outside and blood red and juicy at its heart . . . ' Absorbed by loving considerations of her tastes, Mitzi did not notice that Elisabeth was not replying, and her attention was drawn to her companion only when the peculiar noise of the latter's choking was sounding right round the Hall. Elisabeth's throat had gone into spasm and as she fought to inhale draughts of air she produced only a chilling, inhuman stertorousness. Mitzi tried to rise quickly but her sixteen stones were against all precipitate action. She intended to slap Elisabeth on the back, but she was too late; Elisabeth had made a dash for fresh air and Mitzi's arm met that of Elisabeth's chair. Mitzi was immediately conscious of pain and seconds later of the table upturning and its entire contents spreading themselves across the parquet. By the time Elisabeth was out of the Hall and onto the terrace, the guests at The Tamarisks were all frozen in shocked suspension, their forks lifted halfway to their mouths, their faces pale, their palms clammy.

'Oh dear! Is Miss Danziger dying, Boo-Boo?' The Colonel did not stop to reassure his wife, but rose neatly, pushed his chair under his table and with swift, disciplined steps reached the terrace no more than a couple of yards behind Miss Danziger.

'Forgive me! I'm so sorry! I know it looks dramatic . . . I'm used to it, you see. I must go and apologise to the other guests.'

The Colonel attempted to place a reassuring arm around Miss Danziger's shoulder. 'Are you fully recovered?'

'Yes. Fortunately the spasm didn't last too long. It's the other guests who need your attention. I know it's disturbing for people to watch these attacks.'

'Do they occur often?'

'Quite often. I've become accustomed to them. I know that so long as I don't manage to count up to one hundred before the spasm ceases, I shall live. I count all the time it's happening.'

'Can nothing be done to prevent these spasms?'

'Doctors only deal with symptoms and I know the causes are too deep for them. My body gets itself into a state of refusal. Life "sticks in my throat", I suppose.'

'You are always so tense, my dear. You lead life, it seems to me, like some ritual that demands unerring performance.'

'Doesn't everyone? I mean doesn't everyone have a ritual? It's just that you see mine as being somewhat different from most other people's.' Miss Danziger thanked the Colonel for his concerned attention, indicating her desire not to take the conversation further and her intention to visit the cloakroom before returning to the Hall.

'No, Bo-Bo. Miss Danziger's not dead, nor is she dying. She's powdering her nose.'

Over coffee in the study Miss Danziger thanked the guests individually for their concern, apologised for interrupting their enjoyment of an excellent meal, and explained that so long as she came out of the spasm in less than a minute and a half it was not dangerous and left no ill-effects. Fru Gertlinger sent a message via Fru Møller to say that in future, when there was steak for dinner, she would prepare a more easily digestible dish for Miss Danziger. Until it was time to retire, the guests occupied themselves variously with chess, gramophone records and a comparison of their ailments.

WEDNESDAY

Gulls were holding a revivalist meeting; they shrieked their affirmation from the cliff top and woke Elisabeth Danziger early with their evident enthusiasm. The sleeping pills had left her feeling groggy; she knew from experience that unless she rose immediately on waking, she would feel drugged throughout the day.

Looking down from the balcony onto the terrace, she observed that the cat was undisturbed by the gulls. It lay asleep on a piece of sacking the gardener had discarded from around the rose-bush he was planting. Beyond, Elisabeth watched the sea scouring the shore in a desultory fashion. At the edge of hearing, as she turned back into her room, she could make out the shuffling of crockery.

❖

'I would appreciate a packed lunch today.'

'Fru Gertlinger predicted you would. She has it ready for you, I believe.' Fru Møller set down Miss Danziger's breakfast herself and then turned and called, 'Bertha! Will you bring Miss Danziger her packed luncheon, please?

She'll be wanting to set off just as soon as she's finished her breakfast.'

No other guests were down. Comforting sounds of activity could be heard behind the green-baize door. The scent of newly ground coffee beans and of a huge bunch of white stocks in a green jug in the vestibule filled her nostrils. Bertha's voice, springy and kind, informed her, 'Your tyres were a bit flat. I've pumped them up.' And, with a packet in her extended hand, she asked, 'Shall I put this straight into your basket?'

'Thank you so much!' She would never be able to express how much. 'You're so kind!' Kindness – abundant in the case of Bertha and her mother. 'Yes, please do.'

The road was deserted. Miss Danziger turned off and pedalled along the line of the cliff top. Flights of birds disturbed by the sound of turning wheels rose from their nests and flew straight out to sea. A single tern dropped like a stone into the sea. An imperceptible breeze forced the leaves of a regiment of birch trees into anxious quaking.

The path turned inland and met the road to Sandweg which cut through arable land, punctuated by low, brooding barns. Ten miles distant, Sandweg church loomed into view; it rose from an ocean of grain like a vast liner in the doldrums. Around it, a dwarf cluster of irregular shapes outlined the village that had clung to the church for 800 years. A wind was gathering at the coast, preparing to sweep across the fields, lean against the few trees and race on over the road, across to the far side of the island. Miss Danziger put more pressure on the pedals; she knew that if she did not reach Sandweg before the force of the wind had accumulated its full strength, she would have very hard work before her. The sky was curdling; clouds were forming. The pale sun of early morning was being obliterated and would soon be entirely overcast.

The dominating size and aggressive shape of Sandweg church reminded Miss Danziger that it had played as great a part in the physical defence of the island as in its spiritual well-being; but, although its size and shape were awesome at a distance, the church became increasingly a place of sanctuary as she neared it. It was set in a trim garden girdled by white painted paling; if not God's cottage, certainly not his manor. And as she pushed open the west door Miss Danziger was met by the scent of fennel, the six-foot stems of which towered over her from a huge stoneware pot, very different from the musty scent of piety that greeted her in English country churches.

She sat down in one of the box pews to the rear of the nave. She pulled off the scarf that she had been wearing round her head to protect her ears and prevent her hair getting into her eyes and mouth. She removed her cardigan. She closed her eyes and, as she did so, valves that normally regulated memory burst open. It was terrible: pure pain. She had come to look at the frescos of Sandweg, the frescos that interpreted the story of the Massacre of the Innocents – the slaughter of the male children of Bethlehem at the behest of Herod.

Sandweg church was different from other churches on the island in that its frescos did not bear the imprint of the celebrated Elmelunde master but of some unknown artist who, it seemed, had neither painted nor supervised the painting of any other works of public art. Who had he been? Why had he chosen this subject? For although, ostensibly, the subject of the fresco was biblical, the artist had chosen to illustrate the earlier massacre with scenes from a later, fourteenth-century island tragedy, in which a tribe from the north, with satanic premeditation, landed on Møn with a mission to slaughter its children.

On the first Wednesday morning of every month – with the exception of the months in which Easter and Christmas fell – it was the custom for the incumbent pastor to give his own account of the massacre, or read out an account left by a predecessor. Sometimes the pastor found himself speaking to an empty church; sometimes to a church filled with schoolchildren; sometimes to a congregation supplemented by the relatives of islanders brought over from the mainland, and other tourists. The custom was a celebrated one, and an important aspect of the pastor's work. There had in the past been clergymen who had elaborated the written account in the manner of solo violinists, composing their own cadenzas, and their elaborations had found their way into the written account. There had been others lacking in imagination, who stuck to the basic facts but lent them theatrical weight. Miss Danziger had heard a variety of interpretations over the many years . . .

The pastor who emerged from the vestry into the nave had a file of children at his heels. Miss Danziger judged that the story would be over-carefully related that morning, for many of the children were very young and the more lurid details of the massacre might be regarded as too frightening for them. She did not recognise the pastor. She had not yet raised her eyes to the frescos; she would do so in due course; she found them almost unbearably painful to behold. Instead, she focused her attention on the children as they opened the box pews and, in the case of the young ones, helped one another onto the seats. She noticed that some held hands. All observed absolute silence.

'Five hundred years ago, a tribe of barbarians from the north was ordered by their leader, Gorbrandt, to take to their ships, sail down through the Baltic and conquer Møn, the island they called "The Rich Island".' Thus the pastor started. He spoke slowly to the children and did not take his eyes off them as he spoke. He demonstrated a feeling for drama and a determination to tell the tale so that it would never be forgotten. 'Gorbrandt wanted Møn for the amber he knew could be picked up on our shores. And so that he might ensure that our island would be his for all time, he instructed his hordes to slaughter all the children on Møn.

'Gorbrandt was a coarse killer, but a subtle man. He reckoned that the islanders would be so devastated by the deaths of their children that they would be incapable of taking up arms against the invaders and, later, would be easily subjugated. He was correct in so far as our forebears were piteously shattered but quite wrong in thinking that they could be subjugated. While small, dead and still bleeding little bodies lay like exposed carrion round the harbour, the weeping fathers hovered over them to stop the crows and flies finishing off what Gorbrandt's men had started. Feelings of grief far outweighed thoughts of revenge.

'The humane and futile gestures of our forebears as they kept watch over the dead children had been accurately predicted by the invaders, who sped away, hacking a path through the fields that lay between the port and our village of Sandweg. The invaders' next mission was to capture our treasure, stored in the crypt of this church. We had gold; we had silver; and we had amber. We needed this treasure to exchange against cloth and cattle and spices – and as ransom to exchange against our men when they were taken prisoner in war.

'But clever though the cruel invaders were, they were not quite so clever as they believed. Our forebears were much more clever: they had a secret manner of communication that the invaders knew nothing of.

'Sandweg was one of the seven great churches of Møn. You know the others: Fanefjord, Keldby, Elmelunde, Børre, Magleby and St Hans. Well, each of the seven great churches had a peal of six bells that hung on the outside wall of the church tower. The seven communities that made up the population of Møn in those days ranged round one or other of the churches and each community made itself known to the others in a common language of bells. It was a complex language: not written down but handed down. One might say it was pealed down. It was a language that had never failed; it had no ambiguities; it could cope with all emergencies. For example, it gave news of ships in peril that could be seen from Fanefjord but not from Elmelunde; of fires raging in the forest near Magleby that could not be seen at Børre; of women in labour, requiring the services of a midwife. It could signal the need for food when the rivers overflowed their banks, or for volunteers when snow-drifts were piling up and people were needed to come out and reinforce the banks and dig a route through the snow.

'News of the massacre of the children reached Sandweg a full two hours before the invaders. By the time that the invaders poured across our flatlands this church had been manned and victualled and the women of the parish safely concealed in outlying farms, under the protection of what you, today, would refer to as "teenagers". The youths had been trained especially to protect the women. And, of course, the women took their children with them.

'"Forewarned is forearmed", as they say, and the defeat of the murderous invaders proved easy. Unable to get to our treasure, they were decimated by the rain of bolts our forebears showered down on them from the tower of this church. After attempting for an hour to storm the church, those who were still alive to tell the tale turned back. They were so humiliated to have succeeded merely in killing unarmed children at the port – together with their incapacitated, grieving fathers – and in losing many, many of their tribe, that they set our boats on fire in a final gesture of spite. This way they reckoned that no news of their dastardly cruelty and cowardice would reach the outside world. Once our boats had been destroyed, we had no means of communicating with the greater world.

'Now, if you look around you, up on the ceiling and on each of the arches in the nave, you will see depicted incidents from that appalling massacre.' The pastor moved his arms like windmill sails to make his point. 'And if you were to look in here,' and he pointed to his side, where an ancient oak chest, bound with brass braces and secured with a giant lock and key stood, 'you would find Møn's *Book of Legends*, in which the massacre is chronicled in words by two contemporary survivors.

'*The Book of Legends* contains descriptions of all the acts of heroism that our island people have attempted. Some acts have become known throughout the world, others are known only to us, here on the island. But I have no doubt that all are known to God.' And here the pastor paused for his certainty to touch his audience and arouse their own. 'Perhaps, one day, one of you will attempt something that will merit inclusion in our *Book*. Who knows?'

The children turned to face one another for the first time since the pastor had started to tell the story of the massacre. He had discharged their terror by his final sentence. They turned to judge one another, speculating which of their number was most likely to attain a place in the *Book*.

'We have to remember that story, children. Do you understand why?' It was not a rhetorical question but no child volunteered a suggestion. In a booming voice infused with all the wrath of the Old Testament deity the pastor gave the answer: 'So that such terrible things never happen again!' He paused to consider the effect his words were having. 'All over the world today children are starving, men and women are being cruel to one another and killing one another. They kill, they take away another's life, to get for themselves more than they already have – more land, more money, more prestige. And they kill from spite: they despise the colour of another's skin and resent the way another worships God. One thing is certain and it is this: God weeps inconsolably when man acts foolishly. He cannot forgive man's cruelty to man!'

The stunned children filed out of the church as quietly as they had filed in. The eldest wondered of what God's punishment of the wicked consisted. The younger ones were filled with innocent fear. The pastor waited until the west door closed behind the last child, and then approached Elisabeth. 'I hope you were able to bear with me. I had to tell the story in a manner that the children would understand, but I did not want to risk ruining their sleep by a description of details. The fourteenth century is another country to the young but in any case I don't like to make specific parallels with events in more recent times. I get the occasional German visitor . . . '

The clouds parted and through them a beam of light fell on Sandweg church. It penetrated a stained-glass window, spreading lozenge shapes of iridescent purple, yellow, red and blue on the tiled floor. And then the clouds re-formed over the sun and the colours vanished, like spilt blood vanishes in the dark at the scene of a crime. Elisabeth Danziger's face was drained of colour and expression. Her eyes retreated into their sockets. She had looked up; she had looked around; the frescos left her with an abiding sense of hopelessness, reinforced by the pastor's impotent testimony. In the face of enduring human callousness how can man persist with his compromises? If the pastor himself was willing to water his solution to protect the susceptibilities of German tourists . . .

She did not think to move. She bent over, her head in her hands, and from the core of her being there rose

'*Dayenu*'. The word reverberated round the church and as its final syllable faded on the air another '*Dayenu*' came close on its heels. At first Elisabeth was unaware that the word emanated from herself. Once aware she fell silent, tears coursing down her cheeks. How was it that the ancient Hebrew word had drifted up from within her? She rarely allowed herself to remember Grandmother Gertler but that word was inseparable from the old lady. She had used it liberally – and often ironically. *Dayenu*: 'it would have been enough!' Part of a prayer in which grateful Jews thank God for his manifold blessings. 'If you had only given us the Law: *Dayenu*! . . . If you had only delivered us from Egypt: *Dayenu*! . . . If you had only given me my wife and children: *Dayenu*!' But Grandmother Gertler had her own version and applied the word to less earth-shattering blessings. Had the cook not walked out: *Dayenu*; had it not snowed in June; had her husband not caught a chill . . . Grandmother Gertler had been grateful to her family, but she had been less unequivocal in her thankfulness to God. Elisabeth's face contorted as her mind filled with contra-dictory thoughts. How grateful the Jews have been to God and how sorely treated by God the Jews have been. The old lady was right to turn the prayer on its head. But if there is nothing beyond man . . .

Elisabeth Danziger opened the vaults of her memory and took to her heart her grandparents Gertler, her parents Anna and Jurgen and her lover, Daniel. She called out for their return, she wept convulsively, she implored God . . . And with the cast of her family assembled she commemorated the death of her own innocent.

For this was the day in the week her son had died. He had been born in May 1940 and he died in November of the same year. It had taken many years to achieve the control she had acquired over her conscious mind. Having accomplished this, she had managed to consign the memory of her unnamed son to a Wednesday (the day on which he had been born and on which he had been slaughtered) in August, annually, on Møn.

The birth of her child had almost been her death and his. She would have welcomed both had it not been for her vow of return. A few days after his birth, as she pulled herself to life and became indissolubly bound by bonds of tender passion to the helpless being she had created, she had wanted to kill him lovingly herself. Some atavistic prohibition restrained her. She lived to regret what she regarded as her weakness, for the child's fate was to be so terrible that his existence had to be denied in her own mind.

The camp guards had allowed the baby six months' life and then, when Elisabeth was selected for the officers' brothel and her breasts required for purposes other than those of nourishing a Jewish infant, a non-commissioned officer, having polished his boots, drawn up the mess accounts, written an affectionate note to his wife and son and relieved his bladder, took Elisabeth Danziger's baby from her arms and dashed out its brains against the stone wall outside his office.

Elisabeth had been ordered to stand three feet away and witness the murder.

'Let that be a lesson to you!' the young soldier warned, taking a spotless handkerchief from his pocket to wipe some Jewish blood from the tips of his manicured fingers. And he dragged Elisabeth's limp body towards the camp hospital: 'You must be sterilised. We can't have more Jewish babies; we've got our work cut out liquidating those already polluting our lands.'

I shall survive. I must. I shall somehow come out of this. It can't last forever. The world won't let it go on. They must know what's happening: the Americans, the English, they must know. They'll hear about these places and they'll bomb the soldiers' quarters . . . Decent people couldn't allow these places to exist once they knew about them . . . Ordinary men and women, Germans, will come in their cars, in their thousands, and liberate us. I shan't always be alone and starving. I'll find Mutti and Jurgen and Daniel. They must be looking all over for me. Where are they? Maybe this is a nightmare and I'll wake . . . Maybe I've strayed into another world and I'll get back through a looking-glass. Baby! Baby! My own beloved soul. But new exquisite life can't inhabit such places. It's better that you are dead. Dead. Dead. Life in progress has ceased. Time has stopped. It's all just noise and stench. Shall I ever know what it is to have had my fill? Shall I ever know quiet again? Peace? The sweet-smelling earth? Beloved . . .

The German Commandant had dreamt of a mute Jewish whore and when he was issued one for the duration his cup overflowed.

❖

An understanding had been arrived at with the Danish Tourist Board that nothing of the fabric or the furnishings and fittings in either the Tuscan Villa or The Tamarisks should be altered; the houses had been complete works of art when they were taken over and were to be respected as such.

Elisabeth had not looked into many of the bedrooms at The Tamarisks – in August they were invariably occupied. She had, however, taken every opportunity minutely to inspect the public rooms – the study, Hall and drawing room. The tapestries were in good repair and intact, so too were the pictures and the collection of Bow. The medieval oak furniture, dark and glowing, was said by Mr Hulsby to look as if it were nourished on stout. One or two books were missing from the study shelves; perhaps guests had simply borrowed them and taken them to their rooms.

The German occupying force on Møn had consisted of a single unit, billeted at Gullshaven. Few German soldiers had penetrated to the far side of the island and none had entered The Tamarisks. It was a relief to know that the house had not been depleted and that it remained uncontaminated. Elisabeth never craved to remove items; to take away anything from The Tamarisks would be, she felt, to disfigure a perfectly beautiful body. The house had an existence of its own, one that would outlive hers. The Tamarisks was imbued with the spirits of Anna and Jurgen, of family life and the consolation of friendship. The enemy had destroyed all flesh, but had not discovered the skeleton of brick and its bedrock of soil. Elisabeth would do nothing to modify the arrangement of anything planned and executed by her parents. Her ritual return to Møn was the response to an undertaking, her visits to the house and the sites a reassurance.

After fifteen years she had come to assume that Daniel had died in Auschwitz. But she had never had confirmation of his death, as she had had of those of his parents and hers. Since he had not come back to Møn he must be dead – there could be no other explanation. Their understanding had been quite clear. It had been initiated by Daniel: every year in August they would return. She would continue to do that, for what was alive of Daniel was their past together and her memories of it; to ignore her pledge, to reject their shared experience, would be to complete the work of the Nazis.

Having reassured herself that, so far as could reasonably be expected, no changes had been made in the house, Elisabeth embarked on a tour of the garden. Gertrude Jekyll had not been available to design the garden at The Tamarisks when Lutyens had been drawing up plans for the house, but she was shown these plans and her advice was sought. She would, she said, keep the pleasure garden chaste. Lutyens had been struck by the emphasis she had placed on the word – and on her choice of it; chaste was not a word Miss Jekyll usually employed when planning her gardens, and Lutyens bore it in mind throughout – hence the austerity to which he adhered on the terraces. He passed on Miss Jekyll's admonition to his client.

The wife of the commissioning client was a woman for whom chastity was perhaps the foremost virtue in her repertoire. Its symbols coalesced (with abstinence from all that she desired) around the images of the Virgin, the angel and the arum lily. And being someone for whom an hour on Møn passed more slowly than two weeks elsewhere, she welcomed a distraction; she would plan that part of the garden herself. Unable to draw, the lady of The Tamarisks traced a pattern for a knot-garden from a book of Elizabethan garden design. The paths would be made from bricks left over from the building of the house; the little hedges, not more than twelve inches in height, would be box, and spaces large enough to accommodate blooms would be devoted to arum lilies; the others to gravel.

When the Danzigers took over The Tamarisks, Anna took over the garden. Although she was in favour of keeping the lily garden all white, the awesome echo of Miss Jekyll's 'Chaste!' faded and, in place of unrelieved arum lilies, a plethora of white alternatives was installed. The White Garden at The Tamarisks had become a celebrated feature of the guest-house, and guests who returned regularly brought cuttings and seeds from their own gardens to add to the all-white collection. Fru Møller, who resented the embargo on her taste within the house, and frequently complained of the frustration she endured at having to maintain the past in all its detail, enjoyed the discipline the White Garden imposed, the contacts that it brought her in the gardening world, and the admiration its unusual beauty reflected upon her.

How was it possible, Elisabeth wondered, year after year, to subject herself to these sights, sounds and scents? To be present at the moment the evening breeze shuddered in the roses? The single white anemone set her pulse racing; the suspicion of dew in the bell of a campanula knotted her diaphragm; the fragrance of white tobacco plant at dusk brought tears to her eyes. She fancied she could hear the rustle of taffeta and a man's step: *liebchen* . . . She counted off the names of some of the plants: viola, phlox, petunia, buddleia, mallow, limnanth, morning glory, clematis, gypsophila, geranium, delphinium, *Cobaea scandens*, antirrhinum, scabious . . . There they all were! All in their white form! She breathed in the combination of scents they and other nameless varieties created, aware of the moths hovering above the blooms and the sound of small birds in the climbing shrubs against the wall. Within her a wail was mounting: *Mutti! Mutti!*

Und morgen wird die Sonne wieder scheinen . . .

She could hear guests on the tennis-courts; if she were to walk back to the house now, straightway, taking the short cut, she could avoid them. She would rest before dinner. She would go to her room and take off her skirt and blouse and lie down on the bed. She would draw the curtains; they would cut out the sounds as well as the light. *Mutti!* Unless she were vigilant her silent cry would find a voice. She stuffed her handkerchief into her mouth. If Fru Møller were 'on the bridge' she would conclude that her guest had toothache. Elisabeth walked quickly.

Once in her room she spat out her handkerchief and let her skirt drop to the floor. She caught sight of her reflection in the long looking-glass. Serviceable. Deadly serviceable, the only word for her underclothes. Who designed garments to cover the bodies of women with no expectation of being observed by men? Women, she supposed. Brown wrapping-paper would be as seductive as peach rayon. Peach! Had the designer of the nine and eleven penny range of Marks & Spencer's petticoats ever eaten a peach, ever seen a peach growing, ever noticed the variation in tone and felt the softness and warmth of a fruit ripening against a wall? If

she had she might have been reminded of peau-de-soie –
but certainly not rayon. And why had she bought this ugly
petticoat? Because it was cheap, that's why. What a reason!
Mutti always said: '*Liebchen*, have what is beautiful!'

Elisabeth Danziger did not sleep; sleep did not visit that
late afternoon. She lay on her back in the darkened room and
felt her mind swell with memories. She feared the bounds
of her mind would burst and she would be swamped, her
sanity irretrievable in the flood damage. And, like a drunk
will try to focus on a stationary object to stop him turning, turning, Elisabeth planted a buddleia in her mind and
watched as the purple emperors mated on the white tresses.

'Fetch me twine and secateurs, *liebchen*. They're with my
hat, on the terrace. And don't run: there's no need in this
heat and we have all the time in the world . . . '

❖

Anna and Jurgen, Charlotte and Horst – both sets of parents
had been intent upon creating well-rounded offspring, and
the holidays on Møn, whilst providing an excellent opportunity for the two young people to make music together, were
designed to encourage other interests. The island itself – its
people and their occupations, its geology, fauna and flora,
its architecture – would, it was hoped by the parents, widen
horizons that a too intense dedication to music might
narrow. But it had been Elisabeth and Daniel themselves
who, in 1939, elected to spend the whole summer alone on
Møn, rather than accompany their parents to South America.
They wanted to complete their survey of the island, write

up their findings and take a few definitive shots for their photographic record. They had enough material for a book and decided to offer it for publication under the title *Møn: The Island of Pure Friendship*.

Ironically, the summer of 1939 had been blameless. Clear sunny day followed upon clear sunny day, and when rain fell it fell at night to scent the dawn with the evocative fragrances of damp lavender and box. Fine, dry nights were accompanied by the sound of wild pea pods clacking like castanets. Throughout the season the air had the peculiar resonance that attends hot weather, carrying sound from vast distances.

'One day I shall compose a Møn symphony!'

The two friends stayed at the Tuscan Villa because the music room had two Bechstein grands and the couple were working on duets. And also because Daniel was encouraging Elisabeth to learn to play the lyre and cittern that Horst had recently acquired in Italy. Daniel wanted Elisabeth to accompany him on medieval instruments when he had his repertoire of early songs ready to perform. The acoustics of the music room were especially attuned to the human voice; in fact the existence of the music room had been influential in Daniel's determination to become a singer. He decided that the summer of 1939 was ripe to plan his first full programme of *Lieder*; the two spent hours deciding on the 'menu'. Whereas they eventually came to some agreement over the various 'courses', they argued vehemently over Elisabeth's insistence that the recital should both begin and close with Strauss's *Morgen*.

'But why in heaven's name *twice*?'

'Primo, because it's supremely beautiful. Secondo, because you sing it supremely well. No! Don't interrupt me! You see, by starting with it you emphasise the wholly hopeful, optimistic expectations the words imply and then, by ending with it, you can stress the double-edged sword quality: the irony. It's hopeless trying to plan for tomorrow . . . This way you make the song peculiarly Jewish.'

Political chaos was having the effect of making Elisabeth and Daniel take stock and order their time on the island particularly efficiently. They no longer felt, as they had previously, that there was unlimited time or that things would unfold and develop along the lines that they had unconsciously assumed they would. They felt an urgency to harvest the grain of their experience at once.

'I've made a list: Monday Liselund; Tuesday the museum at Gullshaven; Wednesday Sandweg church and the fossil cliffs. We must check to see whether the lady's slipper survived the winter – only six species of orchids have been seen this year. Thursday the Royal Burial Mound and the other burial places and the port and the primeval forest. Friday Mother Jacobsen and any bits and pieces we've forgotten. That leaves Saturday to spend here. We can put the finishing touches to your programme. I'd like to hear you do Ich Grolle Nicht again and also Erlkönig – they make me shudder! What d'you think?'

They followed the plan Elisabeth had laid. Fru Gertlinger, the young wife of the gardener at the Villa, recently become housekeeper, made them picnic lunches and every day they rode out early to check their notes and make sure that they had missed nothing. They returned late, exhausted. Instead of laying the dining-room table formally, Fru Gertlinger served supper on trays in the music room, so that the friends could listen to the gramophone while they ate. They lounged like Romans, taking it in turn to get up, take off the record, snip the wooden needle sharp, wind the machine, place another record on the turntable.

'D'you imagine that some day someone will invent a gramophone that will play a record with a whole opera on one side, so that we could put the prelude on with the soup and have the finale with our cheese without having to get up?'

On Friday evening, while they were listening to Gerhardt sing In Wunderschönen Monat Mai, Fru Gertlinger burst in uncharacteristically. 'Herr Professor Eberhardt's on the telephone! Come quickly!'

Daniel scrambled to his feet and left the room with all speed. Elisabeth stretched out full length on the couch and listened as Gerhardt related, ecstatically, how her love was unfolding like buds in May. Something unfamiliar stirred in Elisabeth, a profound emotion in which painful longing – she knew not for what – was accompanied by anxiety. At the end of the song she rose from the couch and went to the door, hesitated, did not open it, and then returned to the window-seat. She had not remembered to take the record off the turntable.

The first thing that Daniel did when he came back into the room was to remove the record and switch off the gramophone. The ugly grinding sound was anathema to him. He was shaking, his outlook foreshortened by threat. 'Father says things are really serious. He wants us back immediately. He says we must all remain together. War's imminent!' Daniel paced up and down the polished floor from one end of the long room to the other; his sentences bore the rehearsed solemnity of a stage drama. Eventually he stopped at the window-seat and sat down by Elisabeth: 'He says we should ask Fru Gertlinger and Fru Børre to act as caretakers of the houses on the usual terms until further notice. So I said that instead of our leaving tomorrow or Sunday it might be best to wait until Monday so that I can see the bank manager at Gullshaven; I want to make sure that Fru Gertlinger and Fru Børre are paid regularly. I think I'll make an order in perpetuity . . . It's serious, Elisabeth, really serious. We may not see this place again for a long time.' He rose and wandered nervously about the music room. 'It's awful; I feel somehow that our life, our happiness, our everything is about to be shattered.' Elisabeth knelt on the window-seat and looked out at the ancient trees through the columns of the colonnade. She felt icy cold. She folded her arms about her. Daniel approached her from behind and unwound her arms and substituted his own. 'We'll survive. Of course we'll survive.' And then after a long pause, he sighed, 'But it will never be quite the same.'

Mournfully they toured the two houses, acknowledging with a glance, a pat, or some reminiscence, every object that they loved. The huge arrangements of garden and wild flowers decorating the rooms were in the positions in which Anna and Charlotte would have placed them. It was Fru Børre's and Fru Gertlinger's proud boast that it was impossible to tell, just by looking, whether the families were in residence or not.

'I'm sure they'll always keep the houses filled with flowers. I noticed bunches and bunches of grain and seaweed, marguerites and long-stemmed buttercups drying in the pantry, for winter.'

'Let's hide some of our treasures! It'll be wonderful to have a treasure-hunt when we eventually return!' And each took half a dozen items dear to both and secreted them in places their childhood dramas had singled out as being adult-proof. Finally they gathered their manuscript together. It was a painful decision to leave it behind but they thought it would be safest in one of the tin trunks in the box-room at The Tamarisks.

'I'll ask Fru Gertlinger to have our last films developed in Gullshaven and put the prints in with our papers.'

❖

The bells of Magleby church rang out across the plain. Two motionless, naked bodies lay in a shaft of uncertain sunlight that spread, dappled, over the music-room divan. As the final chimes faded, Daniel raised himself on one elbow and started to outline with his finger the pattern of reflected leaves that decorated Elisabeth's body.

'How beautiful you are!' And he fell back with a sigh. 'How lucky we've been! We've had just about everything: the family, each other, this glorious refuge. Of course, it couldn't last.' And he drew Elisabeth to him. Rather breathlessly, he told her that despite this, no one and nothing could take from them what had been. 'But we must never forget . . . '

The sense of foreboding was invasive. It tinged their love-making. Anxiously, their appetites demanded repeated satisfaction. It seemed that only in their passion could they drown their fears.

'When I sang *Morgen*, I always felt a particular sort of mingled tenderness and passion. I used to think: These are the deepest feelings I shall ever experience; this is the closest we shall ever approach. But I was wrong. Now that we're lovers we're closer still.' He laid the palm of his hand across Elisabeth's forehead and pressed back the curls that tumbled over her brow. 'Dearest, dearest friend. How I love you!' He sank back and started to hum and then quietly to sing snatches of endearments from the songs they knew. '*Dein ist mein Herz, und soll es ewig bleiben! Ich bin auf ewig deine Träume, Blüte meiner Liebe.Vergisst, vergisst mein nicht!*' But his voice was not firm.

Elisabeth returned Daniel's caresses and murmured that she loved him. Neither admitted to the other that each was tortured by fear: now they had more than ever to lose.

'Supposing we do get separated . . . ' Daniel started. 'But it wouldn't be for ever: just for a while, perhaps, and *morgen wird die Sonne wieder scheinen.*' Elisabeth shuddered.

They reassured one another; they insisted that love cannot die. But they did so with the vehemence of the unsure. For what is love to lovers who are torn apart? They uttered unfamiliar words, exchanging for their longheld tenderness their new-found passion. In more exalted language than the everyday, they vowed to remember every blade of grass, every boulder on the shore, every drop of Baltic water that had splashed over the shingle at their feet, and every monument on the island: 'These are hallowed things!'

Daniel took Elisabeth's hands in his and turned them palm up. 'Look!' He showed her that like him she had a long life-line. 'And we shall have a child!'

And they made love again and again, for it was new to them.

'I shall survive. Whatever's in store for me, I shall survive. And so must you. Promise me you'll survive!' Elisabeth clung to Daniel and solemnly promised. 'I have a premonition', Daniel continued, 'that it may be terrible, that there will be danger and degradation . . . But my mind will stay aloof. I shall blot out everything mundane and frightening by remembering us here, together. We shall be making music. I shall be singing *Morgen* – twice over.' He kissed her. Holding her at arm's length he stared into her face as if to memorise every detail. 'Get back here in August, August of any year, August of every year. I shall get back too. That is a promise.'

What can be done on a day that is to have no subsequent day? What can follow such declarations, such experiences? What is the condemned prisoner offered? To choose his own meal and subside into prayer. Elisabeth and Daniel had no appetite for the one and no confidence in the other. They walked hand in hand along the cliff-top path at Møns Klint, and watched the sea. The Baltic lay becalmed that day, yet left no doubt that when aroused it could rage like a maddened beast.

❖

Her eyes felt hot. They ached. Along the line of her brow lay a seam of piercing pain. She recognised the feeling. It would take time for it to pass, and require rest. But she had no time and could not rest: she still had places to visit. Some 100 metres from the church, between the baker's and the grocer's, was a chemist's. She would ask his assistance. In halting Danish she explained that proprietary brands would not relieve the pain. The chemist drew a chair from his dispensary at the rear of the shop and put it down beside the soaps and talcum powders, the bath salts and the loofahs. He indicated that Miss Danziger should sit while he dispensed a potion. She gulped it down, paid the exiguous dispensing fee, and left the premises. But when she got outside and began to rearrange her belongings to fit more neatly in the bicycle basket, Elisabeth Danziger found a bar of fleur-de-lis soap and a cube of rose geranium bath crystals in her hand. She put them under her raincoat in the basket and looked at the receipt the chemist had handed her from the till; there was no evidence that she had paid for these items. Should she return them? What could she say? 'I seem to have done some shoplifting'? Or, 'In my pain I was confused', or what? She decided to do nothing but to throw the ill-gotten soap and bath cube into the sea when she was quite alone. She must not make capital out of her distress, on the one hand; on the other the items were quite small and there was no need to humiliate herself.

She would take the long route back over the desolate flats. The road was unmade, but because it was the only route to the peat bog it was worn smooth by peasants' bicycle tyres and barrow wheels. From it, narrow paths cut into the bog at intervals where the land was firm. Elisabeth stopped at the old peat barge, the single landmark on an otherwise featureless wilderness. It had lain here since she was a child. It had saved lives. For when the mists fell suddenly – as they were apt to do – peat diggers had no other feature from which to take their bearings. There were a couple of diggers far out. Stripped to the waist, one dug while the other stacked. Their barrow full they straightened up and turned to push their way towards the road.

Elisabeth pressed on. At the far edge of the peat bog there rose a peculiar outcrop of limestone. Some of the finest fossils had been found there: ammonites sixty-four million years of age; belemnites – the internal skeletons of a prehistoric octopus; coral colonies. She knew nothing of the dawn of civilisation, but could all too clearly remember Daniel finding ichthyosaurus remains and telling her how they had swum the seas when dinosaurs roamed the land. She had never questioned his facts; he had been ten or twelve at the time and she had confidently assumed that he knew what he was talking about. And he had such patience! Taking a carpet needle or a dentist's pick he would sit on the stones for hours at a time prising small fossils from particles of rock he instinctively knew concealed them.

Elisabeth's head ached. The muscles in her neck felt as hard and twisted as wire rope. As she faced out to sea then turned back to face the land through which she had just passed, her eyes were unseeing; only the past was visible. She remembered watching peasants clear the unworked peat bog. First, they cleared away the living grasses that valiantly pushed at the surface and then the dried stuff from the previous year. Shoots of alder and willow, pieces of old bone, debris swept by the wind – all had to be cleared before the turves were cut. Horst and Jurgen would stand to one side of the diggers and, as each turf was cut and while it was being stacked, they would investigate the hollow from which it had been removed. They unearthed numerous axe heads and sword hilts at this site.

❖

Although Fru Møller allowed that all people had their 'funny little ways', displays of emotion disgusted her. She felt that extremes of grief or pleasure were vulgar, and placed control high on her list of priorities. As a result she was renowned for her ability to cope patiently with awkward guests. Her professional courtesy rarely ran out, even when dealing with the Colonel's wife.

Like many women of small achievement, Bo-Bo was generous with advice: 'Fru Møller, you really ought . . . ' There would then follow a quantity of directives relating most especially to handicrafts – knitting, crocheting, macramé – skills Fru Møller had studiously avoided, let alone perfected. However, Fru Møller did have an interest in wine: its manufacture and its imbibing. Over the years she had developed a discerning palate and acquired an encyclopaedic knowledge of the needs and habitat of vines, the locations of particular vineyards, the reliability of chateaux bottling and the suitability of a wine with a specific food. So when the Colonel's lady – with the provincial's enthusiasm for champagne – questioned her choice of an exquisite and rare-vintage sweet wine from Frontignan to accompany the pudding, Fru Møller was uncharacteristically acerbic in her response. 'I would much rather forgo your interest if it is to be tempered with interference!' she spat through pursed lips.

'Oh, Boo-Boo! I do believe Fru Møller is angry with me!' the Colonel's lady whined to her husband. 'Was I a naughty girl to ask for champagne?' she enquired, certain in the knowledge that children's misdemeanours are not usually regarded seriously. Indeed, the Colonel saw no reason to answer his wife with more than an equivocal smile. However, within minutes, Bertha – who like her mother processed Fru Møller's wishes almost before her employer had expressed them – arrived at the table with an ice bucket, half a bottle of non-vintage champagne and Fru Møller's compliments.

Fru Møller hoped that the Colonel had not registered her impatience. If he had, she hoped her gift would placate him. She did not wish to lose his approbation; the Colonel and his wife were valuable, long-standing guests. But what, she wondered, did the Colonel think about during the periods of his wife's persistent chattering? Why did he remain voiceless while her high-pitched utterances spat themselves about? Were the guests more embarrassed than amused when they overheard Bo-Bo's pathetic chatter? And did the sound of her mastication and heavy breathing, occasioned by her excessive consumption, arouse in them feelings of disgust? These were considerations which Fru Møller weighed carefully.

Elisabeth Danziger was coughing loudly. Fru Møller heard and looked her way, wondering where the coughing might lead. The scent of disaster attracted her like carrion attracts the vulture. She liked her guests to see and hear the efficient way that she dealt with difficult situations. Yet her mind had been so parched by convention that had her full complement of guests not interacted in the manner of characters in a well-made play, set in a small hotel in Scandinavia, she would not have been able to cope. She was always on the alert for a scene of frustration between husband and wife. She was prepared for mild stomach upsets, sunburn and the occasional blister. However, she was not equipped to deal with Miss Danziger's throat spasms. On the rare occasions that they took place in the dining-room Fru Møller's professional know-how and courtesy were apt to desert her. Should she act with sympathy? She felt none, but that was no obstacle to showing a little. Just as she, Fru Møller, was adjusting to the need for a doctor and the possibility of a corpse at The Tamarisks, the same Miss Danziger did the rounds of the tables apologising for the shock and upset she had caused. What was there left for Fru Møller to do? It was being made to feel redundant that brought her to a standstill. It made her flick her eyelids as she passed between the tables. She did this when she had no grasp of a conversation or no understanding of a situation and felt herself *de trop*. Fru Møller was not a silly woman nor was she utterly stupid; she was, however, conventional and superficial. Knowing that Miss Danziger was aware of her limitations made Fru Møller nervous.

THURSDAY

It might have been winter, the sky was so low, thick and grey. The sea was grumous, too. *Und morgen wird die Sonne wieder scheinen* . . . But as Elisabeth stood watching she noticed that where the sea met the shore it broke in lively foam. She too would bestir herself; there was still much to do, much ground to cover, and it was already ten o'clock on her fifth day. She must fetch her raincoat, just to be on the safe side. As she turned to retrace the path to the house, she saw the Colonel and his lady slowly and carefully descending between the tamarisks, through the dunes. They would be bound to detain her.

Bo-Bo was dressed in white from straw bonnet to canvas shoes, and to complete the picture carried an open parasol over her right shoulder. 'Dear Miss Danziger! I observe your face is full of frost, storm and cloudiness! Isn't that just so, Boo-Boo?'

Elisabeth was alarmed to hear the old actress quote – however loosely – from *Much Ado*. Talk of the theatre was normally avoided in front of Bo-Bo because no one liked to suffer the avalanche of tears that flowed when memories of her prematurely terminated career overwhelmed the one-time actress.

'Off to the burial grounds today?' The Colonel's enquiry was delivered as a statement, and he quickly and brazenly continued, 'Odd how man's history resides in his middens. Same's true of the individual, of course: just read psyche for midden.' And so saying he threw a stick into the water.

It is regrettable, Elisabeth observed to herself as she climbed through the dunes, that clever men do not always make consoling company.

❖

It was a long walk, but she felt she needed it. Despite the threat in the sky, it had not rained. Elisabeth was hot; she took off her raincoat, set down the knapsack containing her lunch and some books and sat down on the bench opposite a thicket of hazel, through which a path had been cut.

> Prehistory is everywhere evident on Møn for those with the sight to detect it. Once the ice shifted, 250,000 years ago, nomadic hunters made this region their own – we know, for they left a trail of hewn flint artefacts. By 10,000 BC there were settlements. Today many of these lie submerged by the sea, for the land is flat and the sea has encroached all round the coast. However, in summer our early forebears went inland to hunt deer and birds; evidence of their presence survives in our peat bogs. Here we have found strewn about the animal bones they decorated with their matchstick images of men and beasts, and the skeletons of their boats.
>
> By 3,000 BC early man had put down roots . . .

Elisabeth looked about her. From the slight incline where she sat she could see for miles the neatly sown fields, the healthy crops and the spotless cattle. It appeared to her as if agriculture on Møn might well have arrived with creation itself.

> The New Stone Age saw the introduction of an occupation that was to have vital importance for Denmark thereafter: agriculture. With settled life came settled death. We have the kitchen middens to inform us about the former and the dolmens and passage graves – both resting places and scenes of ancestor worship – to inform us of the latter.

Elisabeth walked the few metres down the path to the round dolmen. It had seven base stones and four capstones; she knew it well; she had been present when it had been discovered and excavated. A sign by its side provided the history of the late Stone-Age burial chamber together with its date of discovery and a list of those who had assisted members of the Danish Archaeological Society on the dig: 'Professor Eberhardt, Professor Danziger, their wives and their children . . . ' And rounding off the formal details: 'Here lies preserved what man conceals.'

She entered the spacious first chamber. There was sufficient daylight pushing in from outside to enable Elisabeth to take her bearings, but she needed the light of her torch to find the entrance to the narrow middle chamber. She lowered her head and entered the Stygian darkness. There was thick mud underfoot; it stuck to the soles of her shoes.

And the air! It was nothing but the stench of dead, rotting rats and of bats' dung. She stuffed her handkerchief into her mouth; it was large enough to cover her nose and for the faint scent of lavender-water to obliterate the worst of the putrefaction. She shone her torch round the gruesome chamber until she found the sodden stone she sought. Black lichen clung to it like rind. With her gloved hand she rubbed and rubbed until the deeply incised ED/DE emerged. Here, inanimate things kept the past intact . . .

It was hard to imagine that *giants* had ever made Møn their home. More likely it had been trolls. Everything was on such a small scale! Elisabeth sat in the open, on the bench provided, and surveyed the countryside. Old Mother Jacobsen had once told her how Møn – 'The Maid' – had been languishing in the frozen Arctic Circle, abandoned by her sun-craving lover, when her cries of anguish had been heard by two giants. Out of the kindness of their enormous hearts, the giants had lifted her out of her icy misery and carefully put her down in the warmer waters where she was to be found today. Rosa Jacobsen had not said where the giants had removed to . . . Doing other charitable deeds in the cause of true love, perhaps? All peasants believed that Odin fled to Møn after the coming of Christianity had made him homeless. They called him the One-Eyed Guest and Elisabeth recalled how, when she was young, the peasants never harvested a field without putting out a sheaf for Odin's horse. Odin was all-wise – but he had not been born so; he had drunk at the fountain of Mimir and had had to pledge an eye. Old Mother Jacobsen would chuckle over this: 'How much wiser must I be than Odin, I who have neither eye!'

＊

Elisabeth was awed by the intensity of feeling awakened in her as she walked through the primeval forest, alone. She felt herself mysteriously attached to the whole of creation. Time here was measured by the moon and by the sun; the forest itself was held in suspension by the river, whose continuous flow sustained its endeavour.

She came to a familiar boulder; it had fallen where the river met the hollow that over the years had become the pond. She rested on the boulder and from it looked down to where the river ran shallow and offered a breeding ground to a lively population of insects. Stinging, biting, their incessant attentions to warm-blooded creatures always raised the question as to their purpose – as if man's comfort were at the heart of the purpose of creation. If she had learnt anything about life it was that no beneficent creator was in charge. Creation had been magnificent and miraculous, but its continuance and maintenance less so. It was as if a genius creator, after six days' labour, had become uninterested in his achievement and had delegated responsibility for the rule and administration of his work to a band of bureaucrats – a tireless bunch of imbeciles, lacking compassion, who justified their role in the scheme of things by ceaselessly inventing trials for man, to keep him on his toes.

At the centre of the pond the water was opaque, a lush green with a smooth surface of tiny plant leaves. The exquisite pattern was disturbed, from time to time, by the sudden appearance of a circle of grey as some water creature came to the surface, displacing the mosaic. The river flowed silently through the forest like blood through the body. The air seemed to be holding its breath. The scent of rotting leaves, beech nuts and bracken combined in a heady *mélange* Elisabeth found intoxicating. She, who was the victim of the harsh tumult of dissonance, observed how the noiselessness of the forest was made evident by the occasional snap of a twig or dry thud of a pine-cone falling to the ground. Noise creates silence! The seeming contradiction reminded her of another: 'the solution posed the question'. Dimly, in what seemed at that moment to have been another existence altogether, she remembered Jurgen and Horst arguing that there was actually something dynamic and hopeful about the forces of good and innocence being so demonstrably at risk from the satanic. Evil in Germany was so heinous, so unmistakable in the late 1930s, that all the world would assuredly join forces to wipe it out. Here was a nice example of the solution posing the problem.

Their friend Otto Korn, the physicist, had shown that particles move backwards in time. Without the emergence of Hitler and his National Socialists all that was rotten in Germany, that had been positively fostered by Romanticism and encouraged by the humiliation that Germany had suffered under the terms of the Treaty of Versailles – racism, social Darwinism, anti-intellectualism, phoney mysticism – might have persisted indefinitely and gradually eaten away the fabric of the country and its culture, gone unchallenged by the forces of reason, lain for all time under layers of sophistry . . .

They should have been more vigilant; a summing up is no substitute for reasoning and judging. Horst and Jurgen had been whistling in the dark. Anna and Charlotte had been arrogant. They had never been observant Jews; they had been steeped in German, not Jewish, culture and identified with it. They did not so much as consider that their physical safety could be at risk. Rumours of the dispersal of families and the deportation of good working stock to forced-labour camps abounded; but this sort of thing happened to other, less educated people . . .

There had been no Jewish community in their city. If there were a few Jewish citizens they went unidentified; there was no synagogue, no kosher butcher. It was not an industrial region; the city owed its origin to a medieval religious foundation, dedicated in the first place to meditation and in the second to study – hence the university. The rich farming land surrounding the city determined the city's development as a market town, with its regular cattle and produce sales, neither of which attracted Jewish merchants.

The terrible times had rendered individuals impotent; many Jews consoled themselves by clinging to any available straw and concealed themselves behind bastions of casuistry. By so doing they colluded in the evils that they would have wished to remedy had they faced them fair and square. By not facing them they were bound to become their victims. The Danzigers and Eberhardts thought that they were choosing their social isolation. They were not. They were ostracised. The unusual closeness of the two families obscured the glare of loathing by which they were surrounded. And they were so contemptuous of the Nazis and their cohorts they could not imagine that they themselves featured in the minds and machinations of such louts. They pretended that what was happening was not happening, and if it were to happen, it would certainly never happen to the likes of them. 'It is wise to bear in mind how vastly superior is the individual over all the political institutions and social mechanisms which oppress him!' They did not know that liberal humanism was powerless in the face of fascism.

How could they have allowed themselves to be consumed? How could they! How could they! The exquisite creation they had made of their own lives blinded them to the aspirations of less fortunate men and women. It was precisely their erudition, their cultivation, their financial security, their disdain for the mediocre that led them to the gas chambers.

Elisabeth watched a snake glide venomously across her path. She walked round the pond to the sunny side where the water's surface was devoid of weed. She wished to know whether the descendants of the trout that used to inhabit the pond inhabited it now. She peered down into the water but was aware only of her own reflection and that of the branches of the beech trees. She lay down by the side of the water and, because the water did not receive her shadowy form, the trout were fooled. They rose to the surface. A shoal of stout brown fish swam round and round in circles in a ghostly saraband before making their way to the entrance to the stream.

The soundlessness of nature impressed and solaced her. She wished to participate in its immutability. She wondered, had man lost the faculty to hear nature? Was it that alienated man was deaf to the language of the hills and valleys, the forests and the shore? *Stumm werden wir uns in die*

Augen schauen, / Und auf uns sinkt des Glückes stummes Schweigen . . .
A dog barked. It was impossible to calculate where or how
far away. The country beyond the forest was flat and the air
still; under the conditions of high summer, noises carried
long distances. A report of a gun sounded; the dog barked
again. Someone was shooting at the fringes of the beech
woods, on the heather moor.

Misfortune engenders isolation. The surviving spouse of
the most disagreeable, friendless partner may find herself at
the centre of a crowd at his funeral, but once dispersed the
crowd does not re-form. Elisabeth Danziger was the sole
survivor of an uncommemorated family. At the war's end,
charity assembled to comfort her for a brief moment and
whilst wishing her long life, nevertheless dispersed and never
reassembled. As the years stumbled by she found that she
had nothing much to say to anybody. She met no one large
enough in spirit to receive a confidence. What was there to
say? The common currency exchanged between strangers
was not worth much. Elisabeth Danziger had fallen silent.

She was a wreck. She regarded herself as having been
battered by uncontrollable forces, washed up in hostile,
foreign waters against jagged rocks. She was maimed; her
mast and sails splintered, torn and partly missing. Her sole
functions – to return annually to Møn, and to acknowledge
her Jewishness. She had pledged the one to Daniel, the other
to herself. All that she could identify as remaining of herself
was the Jew; she would never leave unpaid or transfer her
spiritual account, if for no other reason than that payment
safeguarded what little survived of her identity. Her psychic
solvency depended upon it.

The stony-hearted shore upon which she had been washed up was always in sight of a fretting, dull, menacing sea: potentially dangerous, urged on by the tide, looking for a killing. And the vigorous, life-enhancing breakers that plunged inland, that might have deposited her on soft, rich, regenerative soil, were involved in a never-consummated effort, frustrated by the moon.

She climbed out of the wood by means of a stile and took the path that led round the cornfield. She saw the Colonel coming towards her, his gun tucked under his arm.

'Did you realise who it was?'

'No!'

'Didn't you remember? Bo-Bo did. She said, "It's your shooting day!" Funny what she remembers – and what she forgets!' The Colonel took Miss Danziger's knapsack from her. 'Come! The sun is shining, it's a beautiful day, we'll throw our sandwiches discreetly away and I shall take you to lunch at the Lur Inn.'

It was at least ten summers past that the Colonel and Miss Danziger had met at The Tamarisks and the Colonel, finding the guest a most informed companion, had asked her assistance in helping him pinpoint locations where he was most likely to uncover particular fossils, and attract particular moths. Discovering Miss Danziger to be familiar – even intimately familiar – with every blade of grass on Møn, his curiosity had been aroused. His courtesy, however, contained a reticence that did not permit him to ask outright just how she had come by her knowledge of Møn when she spent only a week a year on the island. The fact that she spoke halting Danish and fluent German and held a British passport led him to conclude that she probably knew the island before World War II. Her name, Danziger, was German. She could be Jewish. And he had once elicited from her the statement, 'I did not have what the English refer to as "a good war".'

Miss Danziger also had it in her favour that she was in all things the opposite of Bo-Bo. First: her appearance. Far from studying it to create an effect, she ignored it. Miss Danziger was not an ugly woman but the Colonel had had to take a long hard look to discover her good features: her bone structure; strong fair hair streaked with less fair strands; her pale complexion, unpainted. She seemed to have the form of an ironing-board, yet that flatness of rump and breast was apparent only, achieved by the unrevealing clothes in which she chose to conceal herself.

And Miss Danziger had the habit of culture. Her taste in all things artistic was polished. She did not depend upon the views of others to form her own, or bend this way and that according to the fashion of the day. He liked that! She was a mature woman. She was unfailingly polite and considerate. She was economical in her conversation. She was unobtrusive. Highly strung, of course; he could see that. Those choking fits, for instance, and the way in which she followed her routine so unerringly. But those were small matters and did not impinge upon the freedom of others.

The Colonel was used to acting in loco parentis and would certainly not have responded as warmly as he had done to Miss Danziger's maturity had he not discerned in it a vulnerability: something he could defend. He could offer her financial security; a home – on Møn; his fidelity . . .

'But our concerns would never coincide!'

They were chilling words and he resented them because he felt prohibited from asking her to explain them. If he did ask her she would become costive. If he nagged, she would beg him not to rummage in her past. 'Above all, don't ask me what I'm thinking. My memories are my memories. They are my treasure.'

'And should you hoard your treasure? Is treasure not like all else: to be used, shared rather than hoarded?'

At the edge of hearing a tethered dog was whining. Above, crows reconnoitred for carrion. At the end of the garden, the waters of the stream that had risen pellucid at their source lay curdled. A heavy stillness ensnared the afternoon.

'Wouldn't you like to remake your life?'

'No. Only reconstitute the past.'

'I watch you set out each day on your excursions. I have the impression that you are pursuing death. Death is a terrible fidelity to maintain. And the past to which you are so resolutely attached – I suppose you regard it as having been ideal? I wonder. The past often appears ideal in retrospect, yet if one looks at it closely it reveals itself as a dangerous place where we laid mines to trap others, and others laid them to trap us. They're apt to incapacitate us in the present if we don't vigilantly sweep them away.'

'And d'you feel you could sweep them from my ground and deliver me from my past – or reconstruct my life without the shards of my past – or what?'

The Colonel put it to Elisabeth that in the autumn of life, simple companionship was as much as one might

114

expect, that a community of interests and a desire to see one's partner pleased could turn what might otherwise be a lonely existence into well-being. Bo-Bo was older than he and suffering from dangerously high blood pressure. She knew nothing of her condition; the Colonel slipped the pills she had been prescribed into her hot drink at night, and she was unaware that she was taking medication. The Colonel would almost certainly outlive Bo-Bo by many years. He came from a long-lived line and was himself in rude health. After all these years of minding a child he would enjoy some intellectual companionship. Elisabeth, whose knowledge and love of Møn were demonstrable, could afford only a week's visit annually. Surely she would welcome the opportunity to live permanently on the island? The Colonel would buy the farm at Børre, and will it to Elisabeth. Svend Larsen had told him that the farm was becoming vacant and had offered to negotiate for it on the Colonel's behalf, the islanders not wanting incomers to buy up farms for weekend occupation only. Larsen wanted him there permanently in his retirement as he was providing not only valuable material for the museum but also help in attribution, identification and so on. And Larsen himself had said how valuable Elisabeth's contribution might be . . .

It was strangely hot. The Colonel prodded the dry ground with his stick as he spoke. 'Would not such an arrangement bring you a little happiness?'

'Happiness? Happiness!' Elisabeth's feelings were in danger of becoming unmoored. She would shortly founder, fathoms deep in torment. *Glücklichen!* The sun was warm on her back and the light sparkled. Within, something was infinitely bleak, unyielding and grey. Urged on by the tide of his insistence, Elisabeth felt herself being swept to the edge of a desolate strand. 'I don't expect happiness!' She had yielded somewhat to the Colonel's insistence. She would not yield to his curiosity.

It had been a good lunch and conversation had been light and easy. The Colonel had recalled exciting nights he had spent in the open, round the naphthalene lamp, enticing and trapping moths; he had enthused over bits of bone he had excavated in the peat bog. Elisabeth was no longer interested in these things but was captivated by the Colonel's enthusiasm for his subjects. And when, lunch over, they had gone to sit in the garden of the Lur Inn and the Colonel removed his jacket, Elisabeth was equally impressed by the pullover he was wearing. The Colonel was invariably festooned in the fruits of Bo-Bo's labours and – if unusual – her labours were most accomplished. The Colonel's pullover had been knitted on fine needles in a macédoine of silk threads. Nothing could have been contrived to accord less well with his lovat green country suit and hat but, he explained, 'She simply insisted that I wear it. I couldn't have stood the scene had I refused – and then I forgot to remove it once I started to stalk.'

'It's most beautifully done.'

'It is; she does these things well – but why the hell does she do them at all?'

Elisabeth did not think that a life sentence of Bo-Bo's knitting was the harshest a man might serve.

'Another man might've attempted to expose Bo-Bo to herself. I've never felt that she deserved that. Anyhow,

I married her out of lust and a sort of snobbism for the theatre in general and pretty actresses in particular. And I had a strong need to pit myself against her many suitors, and win. But she married me out of simple respect. Of course, there are other ways of looking at it: she traded sexuality for material and social advantage. But whatever the case, and despite the fact that she bores me to stupefaction, I can't be unkind to her.'

Elisabeth was grateful that the Colonel had no intention of being unkind to his wife. 'But I can't imagine that your plan for me would enhance Bo-Bo's pleasure.'

'I've thought all that out. Leave the practical matters to me. Indeed, leave all practical matters to me for all time. Wouldn't that lift a burden from your shoulders?'

'No one – nothing – can lift the burden from my shoulders! I live the way I want to live. I agree it's not the way I planned in those remote days when I imagined one could keep to plans. It's simply the way that I've adopted since the plans I laid were destroyed. I walk a tightrope; if inroads are made into my routine I risk overbalancing. So please don't offer alternatives. I intend to keep on going as I have been. As for the past, I have adopted the doctrine of anamnesis. I permit the incidents of the past to haunt me for just seven days of each year. For the rest of the year, for 358 days, I expect my mind to achieve autonomy over my problems and I plod on while life with a capital L proceeds independently of me. I believe that I appear other than I am. I think people – and this includes you – have forgotten the maxim: "tel arbre tel fruit". If I were willing to unstitch the past I'd be attempting the impossible.'

117

'Tell me about yourself!'

'I thought I'd been doing that! You imagine that if I were to catalogue for you the *incidents* of my life, and tell you all my memories, you would come to know me better. And you would feel complimented by receiving my confidences. But such "telling-all" is no more than a form of exhibitionism. Surely you know that, living as you do with a child-woman? Does the kitchen midden swell with pride when filled with undifferentiated garbage? To know another is to *experience* another. This is difficult, it takes time, fearlessness and optimism – it is something I do not propose embarking upon again in my life. And you must understand: to appreciate the pessimism I feel today you would need to have been present when I formed the optimism.'

'It's because you live alone that you're so inaccessible!'

'No! My identity is *dependent* upon my disassociation from others. And I've forgotten what it is to be impulsive. I tell myself that, anyhow, at my age it's more fitting to be self-possessed and reasonable.' Elisabeth smiled, hoping to lighten the conversational tone and distract the Colonel from his purpose.

'Wouldn't you enjoy living with me, sharing in my work?'

'I'm not consumed by any free-floating desire for anything – certainly not an object to serve and adore.'

'I don't feel that you're really explaining yourself. I don't really understand. You love it here, and I could make it possible for you to remain here. Why d'you prefer to return to a treadmill?'

'Well, the facts don't automatically combine to produce the truth, and the truth doesn't make it easier to understand.

You'd have to get rid of a lot of your assumptions before you could fully appreciate why I couldn't live with a man I don't love, or I don't think you could ever understand why I can't accept to be maintained, to put myself at the disposal of another, be in another's company twenty-four hours a day, share another's pleasures and pains – and so on.'

'I think you're simply being disobliging!'

There was no point in prolonging the conversation. There had been no point in embarking upon it. The Colonel always sought her out on the Thursday of her visit, and in the past few years he had, in the most circumspect manner, pressed his suit. He did not approach her sexually; he did not pretend grand passion; he wanted to share his interest in Møn with another who had a similar love of the island. He liked to live in company with another; Bo-Bo had only negative virtues but, he had to admit, he would be lonely when she died, and the doctors gave her no more than a year. She was overweight; she ate chocolates and sweets; she smoked and drank; they lived five flights up with no lift . . .

'Having nothing to lose', he tried, 'is the beginning of opportunity.'

Was he referring to himself or to her? She would refrain from enquiring. If she did ask it would encourage another bout of confidences and result in another round of their sparring. But she accepted that the Colonel was a kind man. He was not to know that because she never spoke about her feelings, she could not express them on demand. She was terrified that one day he might try some moral blackmail and pretend he had come to love as well as respect her. Love: the word would be utterly meaningless in this context; no more than a little blast of sound. No more than a small bullet that would make her bleed. Without being tempted by kindness Elisabeth had registered its existence. But in the end she had come to despise it, observing how easily it could co-exist with injustice, harshness and moral inflexibility. England had alerted her; so many people she had met there affected kindness but so few had warmth. She had experienced nothing but cold and loneliness in the midst of kindness.

'You're imprisoned by the past!'

'And you are mesmerised by the future!'

If she succeeded in nothing else, one thing she determined to do: keep Møn for herself. She would continue to harvest the past annually. She would keep to herself the colour of her days – white Mondays, bordered in yellow, mahogany-brown Sundays. She would chant Morgen silently, and allow the scents of wet lavender and rotting beech leaves to cast their spell. She would live these seven days of re-creation as a monument not only to her vow but to the belief, shared with Daniel, that there are transcendental values in all creation. After what she had gone through she knew she could not reconstruct the universe, only recapture her own lost world. She would never be forced into utterance. She would be truthful but never frank. She would react with silence to the Colonel's inquisitive remarks. She did not want to be rude to him. Apart from other considerations, that would be to show a degree of involvement.

A squirrel skittering on the branches of a lilac drew the Colonel's attention upwards, away from the ground where he had been digging the soil around his feet with the tip of his walking stick. Elisabeth too looked up from her thoughts.

'Shall we wend our way back?' the Colonel suggested.

The sun was so bright, so insistent, it robbed the grass of colour. Elisabeth was reminded of Anna and Charlotte who, on entering a room together, robbed all other women of their existence by their radiance.

The presence of the Colonel walking at her side was dispiriting.

FRIDAY

The road to Elling changed character dramatically at the place where it met the river and altered its course to follow that of the river. It left behind the gentle, undulating pastures and the cows that ambled to the fence bordering them to observe passing strangers, and ran narrow, straight and level about a metre above the river, across the exposed, unyielding marshland. The land had been raped years past by the sea. All that remained on the barren expanse was a deafening silence.

A buffeting wind rushed over the land, bringing with it salt that clung insistently to Elisabeth's face. It was accompanied by the melancholy groan of a fog-horn. Here, the uncaring elements feasted royally, and thrived. Only migratory birds sought out the marshes – in late summer on the way south to warmer climes and in early spring on the way north to breeding grounds. The presence of wading birds was all that defined the place at which the river joined with the sea. Beyond, the sea spread out like a ploughed field; a watery present and past mingled seamlessly. Above, in what appeared a dome of infinite proportion, a timeless expanse of grey hung menacingly over the hamlet of Elling.

Elling clung to a cliff face that lent its dwellings protection from the wind and provided the inhabitants with an uninterrupted view over the sound. The view had a practical function; the men of Elling were fishermen, they had always been fishermen and their quarry had always been herring and eel. But the waters were as treacherous as the fish were plentiful and the women of the hamlet had been stationed on watch for their menfolk since the beginning of recorded history. They sat at their windows or in their small front gardens, making and mending nets and dyeing saffron the cloth for the coloured sails that were traditional on Elling craft. As they worked they monitored continuously the condition of the sea and the sky, the direction of the wind and the length of the day and the night.

In the past the people of Elling had lived communally in a series of longhouses that were not, as now, separated into single family dwellings. Communal life survived until the beginning of the nineteenth century and traditions peculiar to that way of life had lingered into the present. One such resided in the existence of a story-teller: an individual in whom were preserved the history of the village, the life of the community and the lore and legends of the surrounding land and sea. The storyteller of Elling was Rosa Jacobsen.

Old Mother Jacobsen – as she was affectionately known all over the island – was in her late nineties, and she was blind. She had been born blind and her disability had enriched rather than restricted her life. In Elling, sight was the sense upon which most people traditionally depended and hearing was somewhat neglected. Old Mother Jacobsen's unusually acute hearing was likened to that of an animal; and it was valued.

The term 'Mother' had been accorded Rosa when she was still a small child. It referred to the peculiar affinity she had with dumb creatures; lost, wounded and deformed they seemed to seek her out. She had a unique gift for restoring them to health, and an intuition that led her to free each into the wild just when its confidence was regained, its body mended, and its animal fulfilment clearly dependent upon the wider world.

Elisabeth approached the longhouse along a grassy foot-path, her feet making no discernible sound. Yet, even before she pushed open the gate, she saw old Mother Jacobsen look up and the cat on her lap rise and turn before folding itself into a crescent preparing to go back to sleep.

'Who is it?'

'Elisabeth Danziger!'

'My dear, good child! How lovely! I was expecting you, of course, but I must have dropped off for a few minutes.'

Old Mother Jacobsen occupied a third of the long-house. Her portion had been painted apricot, its front door a few tones darker than its walls. Just outside the door, under the window, was a yellow painted bench on which the old woman sat, her feet concealed by a froth of nasturtiums.

'How do my nasturtiums look? They smell very good!'

'Indeed they do! And they look beautiful. I couldn't count the number of blooms. How do you get them to flower so enthusiastically?'

'I starve them, my dear. Did you know that there is nothing they like better than to be starved? It's only by ignoring them that they make a real effort to survive. I'm quite surprised no one has thought to name a variety after Marie Grubbe!'

Sensing that the old woman was about to rise from the bench, the cat jumped from her lap and stood by her side. Elisabeth put her hand under Rosa Jacobsen's elbow and led her into the cottage. The kitchen occupied the lower storey of the dwelling and most of the space in it was taken up by a lemon wood table and four rush-seated chairs decorated in traditional colours and floral patterns. A wide crock on the table was filled with the flower heads, the seed pods and the leaves of nasturtiums from the garden. Elisabeth watched as a bee visited each of the flowers in turn, slowly, carefully, taking its time. A jug of lemonade and two glasses stood by the old woman's arm. She located them without difficulty and poured the cold liquid without spilling.

'Now, tell me, my dear, how are you?'

'Very well! I arrived on Sunday and I've been revisiting the old places. But *you* tell *me*: how are *you*? What have you been doing and what sort of a winter did you have?'

'I've been doing very little, but the usual things have been happening all around me.' Rosa Jacobsen talked of birth and death, weaving the fabric of life at Elling into the familiar pattern of survival and defeat, thrust and withdrawal. 'Only this week we lost the *Flounder.*' And then she told of the particularly treacherous winter that they had had to endure. 'It seems the weather gets fiercer and fiercer as the years pass. Sea-birds froze on the packed ice on the marshes. The wind was relentless: it blew persistently from October to March. And it was penetrating – I can't tell you how penetrating – and wet; it got into all the corners. The shutters were all but useless. I had to hang blankets over the windows at night, and in the morning they were so heavy with moisture that I had a proper job taking them down. I put them on the chairs, here in front of the fire, to dry out and the kitchen was like a steam-bath all winter.' Memory of the event and the inconvenience made her chuckle. 'But you don't want to hear all that!' And so saying, she pushed the jug of lemonade towards Elisabeth and waited for her to speak.

'Isn't that a new picture over the chest?'

'It is, my dear. The artist Tove brought it to me. He heard that the old tray – the papier mâché tray – that used to hang there had fallen and got broken beyond repair and he knew that I would notice the gap. Artists understand: objects have a presence for the blind, and their presence is gratifying and we miss it if it disappears. I asked him, "Tove! What have you painted for me?" and he said, "Shapes loud and quiet, wet and dry." And he hung it there for me and made me feel its proportions. "Is that quite all right?" he asked, and I was able to say that it was – it's almost exactly the size of the poor old tray. "It's the best picture I've done in years, Mother J," he said. Tell me, Elisabeth, what d'you see in his picture? What's it about? Does it tell a story?'

'It's like Tove said: about loud activity and quiet repose. About wet conditions that may be dangerous but give rise to regeneration, and scorched ones that appear daunting but may lead to growth.'

'Others have told me that it shows an old woman sitting looking out on a stormy sea from a tranquil cottage garden. That you see her from the back. They say that there are fish in baskets, and behind the longhouse a field of stubble. Is that a fact? Do they speak the truth?'

'They tell what they see. The truth is more than a recital of the visible. They tell the truth – and so, I hope, do I.'

Elling was perfectly quiet. The loudest sounds were those of the bees foraging in the nasturtium flowers, the deep breathing of the old woman, the crackle of the fire, the light tick of the clock and the creaking from the basket as the cat settled to sleep. Through the open door Elisabeth could hear voices in the lane as she and Mother Jacobsen ambled gently over uncontentious topics.

'Have you always kept the fire going in summer?' Elisabeth enquired.

'I used not to, my dear, but I find that I'm feeling the cold as I get older. Arne comes in from next door first thing and last thing and fills the hob for me, and I'm grateful for the extra comfort.'

With the single exception of the painting, nothing had changed. Elisabeth's gaze took in every object. The cottage was a time warp.

'But you've not come to hear about what's going on *today*. You've come to hear about a far yesteryear and the life of Marie Grubbe, if I'm not mistaken!' And the old woman chuckled. 'I wonder, sometimes, what it is about that woman that haunts both you and me?'

It was a rhetorical question but Elisabeth was pleased to be distracted, given an opening, so that she might contribute to the conversation. 'It was said in respect of her that there are people who seek flowers in the tree of life where others would never think to look – under dark leaves and on dry branches. That is something of what haunts me. "Sunday children, with eyes wider open and senses more subtle. They drink with the very roots of their hearts that delight and joy of life which others can only grasp between coarse hands."'

The old woman settled back in her chair and shook her shoulders as if to free them from the burdens of the present. She took in a few deep breaths, like a singer preparing for a song. She would tell the tale in the idiom of a fairy story.

When old Mother Jacobsen had unlimited time at her disposal and the opportunity to take up the strands from where she had laid them down the previous day or week, she embroidered her stories with meticulous and colourful detail. The local schoolteachers knew that their pupils learnt more from her than from any other source. She could describe weather conditions so realistically as to make her audience shiver or sweat, and children would find themselves taking off and putting on a garment in mid-tale. And she had a way of conjuring up places, in terms of their dimensions, that led those same children to explore their houses and fields blindfold; the dark world that they discovered with their fingertips was new to them – but not frightening as they had supposed it to be. Nor did Rosa Jacobsen stick slavishly to one version of a tale; it was important to her to show how many angles a single event could be viewed from. Stories that did not depend upon a season to make their particular point she would place variously in summer, winter, spring or autumn. Those that did not depend upon the land or the sea she might transpose to another setting. And on each telling she found, intuitively, an unforgettable symbol around which to weave her material. Peasants came

129

to her to be reminded of a particular tale the details of which they had mislaid in the mists of childhood; more sophisticated members of the community, less concerned with the tale than the teller, made the journey to Elling in an effort to keep alive a tradition that had died elsewhere. Whether a visitor came for a particular story or whether the old woman had one in mind she wanted to relate, the preliminaries were the same: she entered into a state approaching that of a trance. The substance of her tale became her reality, and her existence merely the vehicle for it.

Old Mother Jacobsen knew that she did not have unlimited time to tell the story of Marie Grubbe to Elisabeth Danziger; Elisabeth would stay for an hour and then be on her way. The old woman sat silently gathering the strands: the young girl who had known the pain of longing; the rich, beautiful and ambitious young woman who, despite two suitable marriages, continued to be pursued by longing; and the older woman, who found happiness with a poor drunken sot from her father's stables at Tjele. She would confine herself to the final phase of Marie's life.

'The story of Marie Grubbe is not a love story but a story about love – a love that does not depend upon reassurances, whether of a material, emotional or spiritual kind, but is self-generating. This kind of love is so rare as to be almost unbelievable. Indeed, when our great man of letters, Ludwig Holberg, heard about Marie he came all this way from Copenhagen to meet her.

'He found her at the Borrehus at Falster where Søren, her third husband, manned the ale taps and where she ferried peasants and their cattle across the sound. Holberg asked Marie to take him across the water and he left a note about that meeting in his eighty-seventh *Epistle*. It goes like this . . . ' And here old Mother Jacobsen assumed a slightly different position in her chair to render a pompous tone.

'"An example from the history of our own time is a lady of the high nobility, who had an invincible loathing for her first husband, although he was first among all subjects . . . " I should explain, he was the illegitimate son of the monarch, my dear. " . . . and moreover the most gallant gentleman of the realm, and this went on until it resulted in a divorce, and after a second marriage, which was likewise unhappy, she entered the married estate for the third time with a common tar, with whom, though he abused her daily, she herself said that she lived in much greater content than in her first marriage. I have this from her own mouth, for I visited her house at the Falster ferry, at a time when her husband was arrested for a crime."

'Can't you hear from the tone of Holberg's *Epistle* how little sympathy he had for her! And he was incapable of empathy! He had come to question her in the manner of someone who comes to peer at a freak in a sideshow. Few men understand women! But the mistake that Holberg made was to allow himself to be held in thrall by the world of appearances. Marie Grubbe was accustomed to wearing silks. Her father had bedecked her in her deceased mother's jewels. She danced her nights away under crystal chandeliers among the first in the land. She feasted on larks' tongues and sturgeons' eggs and fruits brought all the way by sea from St Thomas. But her days! How did she spend her days? We can only imagine that the long hours between distractions dragged interminably. Marie Grubbe was bored! There is no more dangerous a condition than that of boredom, nor, to my mind, a more wicked one. To be given life and not to serve it or embellish it . . . ' Rosa Jacobsen sighed in disbelief.

And then in rhythmic tones, half-speech, half-chant, she wrung from deep within herself a description of all-consuming love. A passion so intense, a caring so complete as to make all other feeling insignificant. 'It was no effort to find the strength to ferry peasants and their beasts across the Grønsund; it was no hardship to clothe herself in fustian and feed on oats. Marie Grubbe could not take offence at the insults and the brutality to which Søren, her third husband, subjected her when she so thoroughly understood herself and him . . . And to be enveloped in a mist of enchantment was a way of life that the miasma of fashion, affluence and privilege had in no way approached. It was because she had known the contagion of the one that she entered so passionately into the incorruptibility of the other.

'And now, my dear, before you leave, let me take your hands in mine and let me feel your face. Yes, you have grown older, but you have not changed. Let me just say: I remember you and I remember Daniel. I have loved you since I have known you. When all else is gone, love remains. I have a feeling that this will be our last meeting.'

Elisabeth allowed herself to be embraced. She settled the old woman back on the garden bench, amongst her flowers, the cat in her ample lap. She kissed her face. She held her hands. And although the old woman's premonition was an unhappy one and mention of Daniel caused her an immediate spear of pain, she nevertheless felt purged; she always felt some elation after being in the company of the story-teller. Rosa Jacobsen confirmed in Elisabeth her determined quest, not directly, but indirectly, for Rosa was like Marie Grubbe, of whom it had been written that she was someone who 'sought flowers in the tree of life where others would never think to look – under dark leaves and on dry branches'.

The old woman created an aura of sanity and tranquillity. Elisabeth felt serene; accompanied by Rosa's good sense she might well get through the rest of the day without the invasive noises and searing pain that thoughts of the past aroused in her. She looked back at Rosa and her garden. Dwarf-bean bushes grew contentedly beside cabbages, overlooked by climbing nasturtiums, grown to attract the insects that might otherwise attack the vegetables. Yet all was healthy. The old woman waved a frail hand.

The wind had not subsided. Elisabeth took her bicycle from where she had leant it against the garden fence. The lane down to the harbour was steep; the oncoming wind would be of positive benefit.

The ferry was in; it rose and fell on the swelling Grønsund. The gangplank that linked the slipway to the boat shifted to and fro with a grating sound. Before boarding, Elisabeth stood on the harbour wall, gazed out on the wrinkled asphalt expanse and took note of the spume that rose, here and there, from unsettled waves. This was the sound that Marie had rowed. The channel was not a broad one, no more than a single kilometre, but conditions could be rough; they could be dangerous. It was across these very waters that the ex-wife of the son of King Frederick the Third of Denmark had ferried raw men and their beasts to Falster and back. 'One mustn't judge the horse by the bridle,' she used to say.

The Borrehus was long since gone: 'This was the site of the Borrehus from 1705–1731. It burnt down in 1731', the notice read. And over the remains the descendants of the crows, the jackdaws and the rooks that had attended Marie's demise, and later her burial, swooped silently. In perpetuity. If Elisabeth condemned the municipality for not having commemorated a remarkable Danish woman, she blamed Holberg, Blicher, J.P. Jacobsen and Hans Christian Andersen more: they should have known better. Each had used her; none had discovered the essential quality that differentiated her from other lovers. Marie Grubbe had loved Søren Sørensen for the indefinable quality that was his alone: for himself. It was immaterial to her that he was coarse and brutish, that he kept an illegal tavern, that he was invariably drunk, and that he was eventually imprisoned for manslaughter. She and Søren met somewhere outside self, on neutral but hallowed ground, where love ruled and all other subjects were exiled.

Love is a capacity: some have it, most do not. Love is not initiated by or nurtured upon nice table manners, an even temperament, a respectable career, an observance of the law. Marie Grubbe was incapable of not loving Søren; she was neither to be congratulated upon the fact, nor was she to be criticised for it. She loved her third husband like the bird takes to the wing and the sea turns on the tide. Mother Jacobsen had been right! Marie Grubbe's was a story of love.

The path from the cliff top to the tiny bay was still in use by the occasional walker. Elisabeth met no one, for it is uncommon on Møn to meet anyone when out walking. The islanders are industrious; they are either out at work or working at home. Few visitors knew this bay. The path was narrow – only the width of a boot – but it was clear of the marram that grew everywhere around. It was slippery, worn to the chalk, and the drop to the bay was deadly. Elisabeth placed one foot carefully in front of the other, at right angles to the path, and clutched at mounds of grass for support. The gulls that screeched warning to their fellows as she approached too near their territory frightened her, but since this was not nesting time, none spat.

The white, scoured branches of trees that years ago had eked out an existence at a sheltered place beneath the cliff, lay about like pieces of sculpture, fashioned by the weather. For thousands of years the ocean had worked at the chalk cliffs and eventually brought down these trees, and because the place was so isolated and difficult to reach, the branches had escaped use as firewood.

The deeply incised DE/ED made with a red-hot nail was visible for anyone to see. Elisabeth recalled the picnic in the bay; they had grilled plaice on top of a fire in the ashes of which they had baked potatoes. 'Picnic': a word that she had had no occasion to use from that day to this. The world, her world, no longer accommodated pleasure parties in the open air.

❖

Elisabeth chose beer soup to start with, pheasant with grapes and red cabbage to follow and, looking for something light and easy to swallow, wine jelly to round off her dinner.

Bertha set down a tureen for one before her. 'Fräulein Baum asks if you will take coffee with her.'

Elisabeth glanced round the Hall and seeing Mitzi was looking in her direction indicated with a nod and a smile that she would. Had Elisabeth not been resolutely determined to keep her private life private, she might have contributed something with which to shore up Mitzi's fast-held views on men. Although – it had to be said, in all fairness – the Colonel had made it clear that it was Elisabeth's mind that attracted him. If Mitzi had been sitting on the lilac branch with the squirrel yesterday (and at this point her thoughts brought a smile to Elisabeth's face), she would have overheard much to have kept her mind and tongue engaged . . . How was it that the Colonel's assumptions were so unimaginative?

Just as she was taking soup from the tureen and pouring it into her soup-plate the Hulsbys passed her table. 'The cliffs are most impressive, Miss Danziger, don't you think?' Elisabeth finished pouring and the activity took long enough for it to strike her that the Hulsbys were the sort of tourists who only appreciate sites for which postcards have been printed. Møns Klint, known all over the world, as famous in their way as the White Cliffs of Dover, would have been bound to find favour with the Hulsbys. No doubt so too would the Taj Mahal . . .

'I don't like the cliffs, do I, Boo-Boo?' Well, that was something in Bo-Bo's favour! She must be responding to her feelings; the cliffs were overwhelming. Her outfit that evening was also astonishing: pink muslin, in tiers, with a pink-muslin rose pinned on the collar and a pink-muslin bow in her hair. 'The dolls are frightened of heights!' she added, loud enough for everyone to hear.

Fru Møller had started making her rounds, enquiring as to whether the hors d'œuvres were satisfactory. At each table she murmured, 'Will you be taking coffee this evening?' and on being answered in the affirmative added, 'Oh, very well. I have a little announcement to make to you all. Instead of telling you individually, I shall wait until you're assembled. The study has a more intimate feel about it.' And she swept gracefully on.

Elisabeth was seated by Mitzi Baum on a sofa designed for three but amply filled by her thin form and Mitzi's generous one. She was continuously anxious lest Mitzi upset coffee all over them both – the coffee-cups being very small, and seeming almost doll's size in Mitzi's hands. When the older woman strained to attract Fru Møller's attention for more coffee, Elisabeth was sure that she could hear seams ripping apart and press-studs popping. Her thoughts were interrupted by the unusual sight of Fru Møller stationing herself in the middle of the study and clearing her throat.

'My colleague, Fru Blicher, at the Villa has asked me to extend her best wishes to you all and invite you to a *Lieder* recital to be held in the music room – you know, that lovely room with its medieval instruments – tomorrow evening.' There was a murmur of pleasure. She went on: 'Fru Blicher has among her guests a South American singer. He arrived late yesterday afternoon, it seems, and he has offered to give a little recital to anyone on the island who wishes to attend. I just hope there won't be too many . . . the music room can only hold about a hundred, comfortably. Mr Larsen has been roped in to see that all the music lovers of Gullshaven are informed – I know that the doctor and the pastor and one or two of the schoolteachers are devoted to music. I'm sure they'll want to be with us. I have to admit, we don't often get such an opportunity on Møn. I understand that the singer is a very celebrated one in his own country. That's reassuring. If there's one thing worse than a poor singer, I don't know what it is . . . ' And Fru Møller looked round the company for their assent.

'Do we know what he intends to sing?' Mitzi Baum enquired to the evident disapproval of Fru Møller, who could see a gift-horse being looked in the mouth at one hundred metres.

'We do not!'

'I shan't go. I don't like song-singing, not the German sort,' the Colonel's lady confided.

But her husband was insistent. 'It'll be a delightful distraction and I would appreciate it if you came along!'

'Alright, Boo-Boo. Just for you. And I do like to watch performers, don't I?'

Elisabeth listened to this exchange with interest, impressed by the Colonel's consideration and his wife's capacity, despite her silliness, to make a fine distinction.

'And Miss Danziger? May we count on you?'

'Oh, indeed! I should like to attend.'

'Fru Blicher is laying on a cold buffet for the audience and performers after the recital and we shall be introduced to the singer and his accompanist. It should be a most memorable occasion!'

SATURDAY

Elisabeth Danziger stood at the open window and watched the gulls swoop round the house, fly straight out to sea and then drop suddenly for prey. On the corrugated pewter there floated two boats. She wondered whether they were anchored; they seemed fixed; they did not bob. Curious, how seabirds do not sing, but moan and shriek, always at war or in pain.

> The sad sun
> In a sick doubt of colour lay
> Across the water's belt of dun.

The last day was always the most difficult. She did not want to pack her few things. She did not want to prepare to leave. She felt depressed. Yet was she not always depressed? Why was she particularly conscious of it today? Depression – like creative work – does not take place in the interstices of life: it is continuous. It is a mode of being. One chooses: to be a depressive or to be creative. One or the other. Or *does* one choose? Can one choose?

My soul is dry! I assume I have a soul, but do I have a soul? Perhaps not, for to have a soul the psyche must be fulfilled . . .

She used to return year after year in the hope that one day Daniel would keep his appointment. She had long since abandoned that hope. Nowadays she returned to defy the enemy: to keep her vow. She must not give in. If she could no longer rise to an adventurous life of the spirit, she could keep doggedly on. The doctor provided her with antidepressants. He could only regard her existential pain as a cup of instant coffee to be sweetened with saccharin.

She walked along the corridor and opened the door into the minstrels' gallery. She had not looked in on the gallery this visit. Below, in the Hall, Fru Møller, Fru Gertlinger and Bertha stood in a huddle by the sideboard, talking in low voices. She caught a few words but did not hear Fru Gertlinger say, 'It would be best to say nothing, I think. It would be too intimate: an imposition. But I'll write a little note. I'll hint. You can give it to her this evening, just before you set out. That way Miss Danziger won't have too much time to consider the implications.' Fru Gertlinger was a tactful woman, and warm. She was spontaneous, not like Fru Møller. She was motherly! That was it. Elisabeth valued her consideration. Fru Gertlinger knew that Elisabeth did not want to unpick the past with her and she never made mention of it. But she remembered things: what Elisabeth liked to eat, for example. In all the packed lunches she put together there was invariably an item included that only someone who had known her long ago, before the war, would have troubled to include.

'It's going to be a terrible shock!' Fru Møller said.

'It may be a lovely surprise!' Bertha was constitutionally optimistic.

Elisabeth backed out of the gallery. Clearly, the conversation was a private one. She had caught the atmosphere of tension but not the substance of the conversation. She hoped no one had noticed her. She did not want to appear to be eavesdropping. She returned to her room.

What should she do? She could not spend the day looking out of the window. She would walk into Stege. That would take a good hour and kill the time. She needed shoe-laces . . .

She found herself in the public library. Being a Saturday morning the library was full of children quietly selecting their books, taking them into corners to try them out before deciding which to take home. Elisabeth watched them: watched herself watching them. Embarrassed, she drew from a shelf a book on Møn.

Eighty per cent of the land is under plough . . . no railway . . . difficulty in attracting new industry . . . Møn's most splendid period dates from 1326, when the Baltic and Sound were world trade channels and the herring, according to the thirteenth-century Danish historian Saxo, could be scooped from the sea with bare hands. By 5,000 BC men were living along the coast; they hunted and gathered mussels. By 3,500 BC they had settled with livestock; they grew barley and erected dolmens . . . In the seventeenth century the island was mortgaged to a Dutch merchant . . .

141

Møn had a history! Would it have an independent future? Elisabeth could not imagine it changing much. It would be good to live here permanently, at the farm near Børre. But not with the Colonel – nor at the instigation of anyone else. Perhaps, yes, most certainly, she would live here if she could afford to do so . . .

She walked by the river. The herring fleet was moored well inland, and the water was oil-tarnished. It was as if the fleet were nesting . . . By the side of the towpath, grasses with long brown tassels bowed their heads in recognition of the fleet's pre-eminence. Dust blew; it was getting into her eyes. She rounded a corner quickly; in a tiny estuary the small boats of the eel pickers were congregated. She had forgotten about them. Before the war she had gone out with those fishers and watched them spear their quarry by torchlight in the early hours of the morning. She walked past the sugar-beet factory and the egg-packing plant and the offices of the Møn *Gazette*. No one was abroad. She would walk on to Marienborg.

Had she been asked to account for her day Elisabeth Danziger would have been unable to do so. She ambled down roads and along paths that she knew well and she failed to record what she saw. Everything upon which her eyes focused was obscured by a heavy veil. It was hard to go on; hard to survive only to survive. Hard to return for seven days and in those days churn up the past and curdle precious memories. And she had lost the ability to see the world without being aware of being aware of it. Beauty had become an abstraction; she was never caught off-guard by it.

Mutti . . . Jurgen . . . Daniel. Had it been a dream?

Along the path by the side of the warm regenerative earth she caught sight of blue waves. The sun was shining. The fields were silent. Only the *Glücklichen* were absent . . .

'Miss Danziger, I'm so glad I caught you. We shall take tea at six. Does that suit you? I thought that since the recital is to start at 7.30 you might all like something a little substantial before we set out. We shan't be having Fru Blicher's buffet until well after nine . . . ' Fru Møller was at her organisational best. But she was feeling guilty: she had not given and she would not give Miss Danziger Fru Gertlinger's note. Her duty – a duty in which she took consummate pride – was to ensure the smooth running of The Tamarisks. Whatever effect Fru Gertlinger's hint had on poor Miss D – and it was impossible to forecast just what it might be – it would be upsetting. Any upset was better confined to the Tuscan Villa, where Fru Blicher officiated.

'I'm going to have a rest now, Fru Møller, and I'll be down as near to six as I can make it.'

And at 6.15 Miss Danziger entered the drawing room, where at least eighteen of the guests were gathered drinking tea and eating from a selection of Danish pastries and pies, and talking with unusual excitement.

❖

The music room had not changed. The parquet floor was bare and highly polished. Along one wall the old tapestry looked undiminished by time. It had been destined for the pinacotheca but the dealer had had a soft spot for

Charlotte . . . The oak refectory table, which sat thirty and came from a monastery in the Tuscan hills, had been moved near the door to the kitchen. Fru Blicher had organised eighty chairs from a nearby school and set them in a semi-circle round the platform. The antique musical instruments had been stowed away in the glass-fronted cabinets. The couches and armchairs had been moved into another room. The crystal chandelier sparkled.

Elisabeth had not walked over to the Villa with the other guests, but lagged behind. 'Yes, I'm coming, but I've one or two things to attend to first,' she explained. And when she did at last enter the music room – through the door from the arboretum – she found herself a seat at the back, at the end of a row. She had taken pains to arrive only just in time. Fru Møller, seated in the front row, was too busy being pleased at this opportunity to provide her guests with free, unexpected entertainment to think of much else. She had looked round once to see if her guests were all in situ and observed that almost all the chairs were occupied. She smoothed her unwrinkled silk dress, fingered the amber beads at her neck and settled into her chair, determined to experience herself being well-pleased. Elisabeth noticed Bo-Bo and the Colonel were stationed third row centre. Bo-Bo was managing to hold her tongue. Mitzi was magnificent in magenta. The Hulsbys were present – but insignificantly so.

And then the lights of the chandelier dimmed. Only the lamps on the side-tables were left lighted so that the room appeared oceanic, bounded by small islands. The door to the platform opened and Fru Blicher entered followed by a much younger, unusually beautiful young woman and a man at least fifteen years her senior carrying a sheaf of music. The man stood the music carefully on the rack and watched the woman settle on the stool.

'I have very great pleasure in introducing to you all Herr Eberhardt and his wife. The Eberhardts have come all the way from Rio!' A murmur of surprise rose from the audience. Among the guests there were those who remembered the singer and his parents. Audible gasps rose here and there together with short, whispered words and the murmur of anticipation. Fru Blicher continued, 'We've not had time to print Herr Eberhardt's programme – in any case, he wants this to be a somewhat informal occasion – so Herr Eberhardt will introduce each of his songs himself. I would like to say on behalf of us all how glad we are to welcome the Eberhardts, and how privileged we feel ourselves to be offered this recital. May I present: Daniel Eberhardt!'

Elisabeth heard the words but did not take them in consciously. She looked at the singer and his wife as if from the wrong end of a telescope. She was aware of a feeling of acute pain; she was in panic; she was terrified that she might scream. She was not altogether sure whether she was dreaming. She pinched her thigh.

The man was like Daniel. She remembered that walk: it lacked caution. He was going to speak. She must get out. She thought to move but nothing happened; her legs did not respond. I'm dreaming, of course! He was coming to the edge of the platform. He was going to speak!

'Good evening! I'm delighted that you've been able to come along at such short notice. Let me first ask your forbearance. I used to speak Danish, I no longer can, so I'm going to have to address you in German – the language of my programme. This is the first visit that I've made to Europe since my escape from Germany in 1940. It was my Brazilian-born wife – who you see is my accompanist – who insisted we accept engagements in Europe because she wanted to see where I grew up. I decided that we should come here first – to the house that was my parents' summer retreat, near that of my aunt, uncle and cousin. Next week I shall take my wife over every inch of this lovely island, which I and my cousin consecrated many years ago, when our destiny seemed assured and likely to be shared.

'In the summer of 1939, just before the outbreak of war, my cousin and I planned, in this very room, what was to have been my first *Lieder* recital. It was a programme that I was never to perform – until tonight. I am the sole survivor of my family. I owe my physical survival to the courage and compassion of the Quakers. But I owe my life to music. Møn was an idyll for me, one enriched for its being shared with my cousin, who was my closest friend. Because my first experience of love was here, I have never wholly transplanted myself from this soil. Indestructible bonds were forged here, linking me to her, to you – the islanders – and your island. The ground of my being, the cornerstone of my art, is here on Møn, pre-dating the destruction of what I loved and those whom I loved. The might of the Nazis cannot destroy memory.'

Daniel Eberhardt walked over to the piano. His wife passed him a score. 'My first song is *Morgen*. And I shall

146

also conclude with it. The words are by a Scot, John Henry Mackay. The music is by Richard Strauss.'

Silence crept into the music room. The piano introduction to the song washed gently over the audience and carried them in its undertow towards glorious possibilities. As the deep velvet baritone quietly affirmed '*Und morgen wird die Sonne wieder scheinen* . . . ', a hawk moth, disturbed at the window pane, raced towards the bulb of a reading-lamp and dashed itself against the light until it fell exhausted on to the table. A single rose in a specimen vase, responding to the almost imperceptible impact of the moth, dropped its red petals noiselessly by its side.

No one saw Miss Danziger leave. Her absence was registered by Fru Møller at about ten o'clock and she did not mention it to anyone. She fully accepted that the appearance of a member of her family she believed dead would be something Elisabeth Danziger would wish to experience alone.

❖

The recital had been a remarkable musical occasion and the audience, comprised both of visitors to Møn and residents of the island, had felt united and at peace under the spell of Schubert, Schumann and Strauss. The singer was hypnotic; his voice resonated in the breasts of his audience, many of whom were moved to tears. And his young wife accompanied him with a sensitive mastery that could only have been born of love.

Early Sunday morning a fisherman walking his dog found the body of Miss Danziger at the foot of the pier where his boat was moored. Had it not been for the empty little bottle in the pocket of her skirt – which could so easily have been swept away by the waves – the fisherman's description of the likely accident would have satisfied everyone.

> And tomorrow the sun will shine again
> and on the path we walk in our happiness
> it will again unite us
> in the midst of this sun-breathing earth . . .

> And to the wide shore with its blue waves
> we shall again descend, slow and still,
> mutely we shall look into each other's eyes
> and the silence of happiness will again sink upon us . . .